It Ain't Always Easy

IT AIN'T ALWAYS EASY

Kathleen Karr

FARRAR · STRAUS · GIROUX
New York

Copyright © 1990 by Kathleen Karr
All rights reserved
Library of Congress catalog card number: 90-50452
Published simultaneously in Canada by HarperCollinsCanadaLtd
Printed in the United States of America
Designed by Alice Lee Groton
First edition, 1990

For Suzanne and Daniel—
because they asked for it

And for Cathy and Trish—
because they fought the battle with me

It Ain't Always Easy

Chapter 1

MY HOME AIN'T much, but I'm 'ordinately
fond of it. It's down in the basement of Huffmaier's
Bakery. One of those little cubbyholes next to the coal
chute, right behind the big brick oven. It's hot as Hades
in summer, but toasty in winter, and passable rest of the
year. I got it fixed up nice as you please. There's a stone
shelf for my candles and cigar butts, my mat and blanket
ain't too lousy, and I papered over the rough bricks of the
wall with the *Police Gazette*. Not every soul's got good,
edifying reading matter right there when he's wanting it,
either. I already memorized most of the top wanted crim-
inals in New York City, like Oscar Burns, pickpocket
and burglar, known for the pearl in his right eye, or Paper
Collar Joe, bunco-steerer par excellence.

I'd know 'em all, if ever I came face to face with them.
Not that there ain't plenty more, unsung, working for
Tammany Hall every day. But that ain't what you need
to know right now. Right now you're probably wondering
how it is I come to be at Huffmaier's. Well, I could've
moved in just as easy over at Flynn's Bakery, but somehow
soda bread ain't got the same consistency as a good hunk

of German rye. Or take old Fred Huffmaier's black pumpernickel. Now, that's bread to put body in a man. Guess I figured I needed some of that body, since I been hovering near four foot for most of a year now.

Old Fred ain't really that old, not gray-headed or anything, but thickset and strong from bashing all that dough around every day. He lets me stay here in return for I shovel coal and clean out the ashes. For that I get my room and as much stale bread as I can stomach, although I must say I been known to lift an occasional fresh loaf or kaiser bun hot out of the oven when his back's turned. Tastes better somehow all warm and soft that way. Just a pity he ain't got a brother in the butcher business. A nice sausage would go down good with the bread sometime.

Well, old Fred's got a mean temper. That's why I use the coal chute mostly for my comings and goings, to keep out of his way. He's clattering around out there by the oven now, fixing up for his morning bake, and I can feel a temper coming on, just by the way he's muttering to himself in German. In about a minute he'll be shouting up a storm, but in passable English (he speaks it as good as me when he's a mind, on account of his being born right here in America, same as me). His wife must of come home with one of her new hats again.

"Jack! Jack-you-young-scoundrel!"

It ain't always convenient being your sole support. Guess it's time to drag my body off the mat, have a quick peek round the oven.

"Jack McConnell!"

It must be Saturday. He's shaved off his week-old beard, but didn't yet take the time to slick down his rough yellow curls. They're still sticking every which way from sleeping. And his big nose is already dusted up with flour, likewise the red long johns. Ain't even pulled the suspenders of his britches up yet.

"Yes, sir?"

"Look sharp with the coal, or I'll cuff you one. The heat ain't up enough yet, and here it's almost four of the morning."

"Yes, sir."

I went for the shovel, a big 'un, taller than me. This old shovel and me, we been through lots together. Must be close on two years already. Took me a little time to settle down at Huffmaier's after the whole family got taken off with the diphtheria like that, and me, the oldest child, barely eight. Guess I spent maybe half a year out on the streets, shining shoes, selling the papers, before I wised up. Of course, I still do a little of that for spending money, after the baking's done for the day. Guess I even stole an apple or two during those first months. I never enjoyed their taste much, though. I kept thinking what my ma would of said. She always wanted the best for us. Even taught me to read and write in between her hours of stitching and washing and cleaning. Said we ought to make something of our opportunities in the New World. Trouble was, everything she made, Pa just took and drank away. He didn't do it meanly, more sort of dog-in-the-manger-like. He'd just say it was the Irishman's curse, and there wasn't nought he could do about it now. But I don't know, if he'd had a little more spunk, maybe it could've been better. I always figured I had more of my ma in me anyhow. That's why, after they were all gone,

5

I took her name. Maybe I'll do better as a McConnell than as a Kelly.

I just managed to dodge the hairy paw that reached out for me.

"Doing more of your thinking, boy?"

"Sorry, sir."

It was deep New York winter. We weren't but twenty-odd days past the New Year. 1882. I thought about it as I climbed out of the chute and paused to brush coal dust from my jacket. Have to find a new one soon. This one rose up two inches past my wrists and hardly buttoned anymore. Maybe I had grown some, after all. I reached back behind me for my kit.

"Jack! Psst. Jack!"

"That you, Mandy?"

I turned to find a pinched, pale girl hiding behind the garbage pile. We'd got to be close of late. She'd only just taken to the street before Christmas and didn't know the ways of it yet. On real cold nights I snuck her down the chute with me.

"You said you were going back to your pa, Mandy."

"I thought and thought, Jack, but I just can't do it. I'd rather take my chances out here than with his beatings."

"Come here then, I've something for you." My pockets had come to take on lives of their own, stretching to hold all sorts of treasures. Now I pulled out a sweet bun. I wouldn't of cadged it for me, mind you, least not this morning with him in such a humor. But she needed some looking after. It was snatched from my hand.

"Oh, Jack! It's still warm!"

I smiled. Her eyes lit up so nice when she was happy. Reminded me of my little sister Becky, the one I always teased before I knew better, before it was too late.

"You want to come with me, then? I've got my shine kit. I'll teach you how."

"Oh, would you?"

She blinked her long lashes at me. Women. Now that I'd offered, I guess I was stuck.

"Where'd you sleep last night, then?"

She skipped up next to me, and stayed there, right out of the alley.

"Underneath a fish stand." She wrinkled her nose. "It smelled awful. And I had to clean out the scales and things first. But I bundled up with lots of old papers like you showed me."

"Good." I looked up at the sky. It wasn't comforting. "Snow's coming, Mandy. You better keep close today and stay with me tonight."

"Yes, Jack."

She said it so trustingly, like she knowed there wouldn't ever be any trouble with me around. Now I'd really done it. I'd never get rid of her.

I led the way uptown and finally set up shop in front of the Union Club. It was at Fifth and Fifty-first, so it was a good hike. Would have been easier if we'd have taken the horse bus, but that was seven cents apiece. Didn't have that kind of cash to be throwing around for a luxury. I liked to work in front of the Union Club, though. Lots of rich men, and men wanting to be rich, went by here. It was a good place for business.

Well, it didn't take long before I figured out that Mandy

might never make a top shoeblack, but she sure knew how to gather clients. A fine gentleman would alight from his carriage and she'd just go right up to him and flap those eyelashes prettily. Concentrating on her, he'd step right in a puddle, and next thing you know, I had a customer. Business was never this good. In fact, it was so good that after a few hours, when my fingers were turning blue under the almost permanent coal dust and blacking, like they did in this weather, I decided to pack it in.

Mandy stopped me. "Wait. Just one more cab."

"You know something I don't, girl?"

"Just a feeling, Jack. They come over me sometimes."

A hansom was just pulling up. A stout young man began edging out, and Mandy went to do her turn. Lashes, smile. "Shoeshine, sir?" Puddle.

Our latest victim pulled his boots out of the puddle with a look of chagrin. "Possibly yes, young lady."

I hove to with a will. Nice-looking boots, these. Hand-cobbled. I made them sparkle with my blacking.

"How much, young man?"

"A nickel?"

He peeled off one glove, revealing a pale, glittering jewel set in heavy gold on his ring finger. He fished under his greatcoat and into his waistcoat pocket. A flash of gold flipped toward me.

"But I haven't change, sir."

"Think big, young man, think big. A word of advice from Diamond Jim."

"Yes . . . Yes, sir. Thank you, sir."

He'd hardly sauntered off when Mandy was down next to me, staring at the coin. "What is it? I never saw anything like it!"

I packed up my kit. "A ten-dollar gold piece, Mandy. That's what it is. How'd you know?"

"Know what?"

"That it was coming?"

"Something just told me to wait, Jack."

"We'll not wait any longer." I took her by the hand as the first flakes of snow drifted down.

"Where're we going?"

"To celebrate."

Like royalty we waltzed into a fine dry-goods establishment. Tall, disapproving faces stared down at us. Mandy's blue fingers squeezed my blackened ones even harder. I recognized a personage who had to be none other than the floorwalker head hastily toward us.

"Out, out! I'll have no ragamuffins warming themselves in my store!"

I stood my ground and flashed the gold piece. "We've come to make a purchase, sir. If you'd kindly lead us to the gloves? Leather gloves."

He backed off. "Pardon me, young man. Right this way."

Like royalty we were led to a counter and fitted. From there we went to boots. Mandy's were still passable, but my toes had been protected by nothing but newsprint for some months. The new ones squeaked a bit, but felt just fine with the new woolen socks. As one clerk walked away holding my holey old socks in front of him like they carried the plague, I topped off our purchases with thick scarves for both of us, and there was still money left.

When we left the store, the snow was falling hard, but it would not stop me. I'd been waiting for such a moment for too long. A bookseller's was at hand. Inside I purchased one of Mr. Dickens's tomes and had it carefully wrapped up with brown paper and string against the weather. We ran then for home, hardly able to see before us. The snow was already several inches thick on the ground. It was going for a blizzard.

With Huffmaier's close, I pulled Mandy into an eatery and we dined on pea soup, thick fried potatoes, and steak. That man had told me to think big, and I did. My last penny bought us each a peppermint stick on the way out. I dangled the candy jauntily from my lips and tried to shove my stomach out the way that Diamond Jim's had. But I guess it would take a lot more gold-piece bonanzas, on a regular basis, before I achieved that effect. Still, it had been a prime day.

As we turned into Huffmaier's alley, I could barely find the coal chute. It was covered by a foot of snow. I shoved the snow away and ushered Mandy through the opening, feeling smug. Let it storm forever. We were safe.

Fred Huffmaier didn't make it down to the oven for five days. It must have still been snowing. He'd never missed a day before. But I kept the oven stoked in any case. It was either that or freeze. Couldn't see anything out the tiny cellar windows, but you could feel the cold right through the bricks and pink sheets of the *Police Gazette*s in my hole.

Mandy and I, we were happy as clams in the bay. When we were hungry, we got into old Fred's baking supplies. That oven fried up his eggs fast, and they went down well with toasted crusts and his jug of cold milk. I borrowed victuals I'd never before dared to touch with new impunity. The worst he could do was throw me out after the storm. And that looked to go on forever. There was no way we could get out of that basement by either the chute or the street-side door. I'd tried, and they were blocked solid by snow. We were stranded good and proper, which gave us plenty of time to get all the way through my new book, *Oliver Twist*, and some left over to talk. We did a fair amount of that, too.

"There's more winter coming, Mandy, and I can't keep you down here with me forever."

"Why not, Jack? It's so cozy and nice. I can't remember ever being so happy."

We had set the mat and blanket in front of the oven, with Fred's kerosene lamp to spark up the dim glow from behind the closed iron door. She was snuggled up next to me, like a cat, while I read aloud. I almost snorted, then stopped myself. It was kind of nice this way. Like having my own family again. I looked at her hair. It was different, clean. We'd had a good wash-up in Fred's rain barrel, even used his soap to scrub our heads. Now Mandy's hair was its true color, warm brown, with little glints of red in it that brought out the blue in her eyes. It fell down past her shoulders in soft waves. She'd said I looked strange clean, too. Said she'd never knowed my hair was wheat-colored beneath the coal blacking. I guess I'd forgotten about that myself, although I never would of called it wheat. I guess "yellow" would come close enough to my mind.

Mandy even had to remind me my eyes were green. A fellow doesn't have time to think on things like that. More important is to grow bigger and stronger than the other guys so I can lick them in a fight. But maybe I ought to scare up a bit of mirror for my room after the storm and try to fix myself up a little once in a while. It might be good for business.

"I guess you're right, Mandy. It is cozy and nice." I sighed and picked up the book again. I especially liked the part where the hero comes into his fortune and doesn't have to be an orphan anymore. She must have been thinking the same thing.

"Do you think, Jack, that maybe my pa isn't really my pa? You know, maybe I got left with him by mistake when I was a baby? There might be a rich aunt or uncle out there waiting and searching for me this whole time. They may have been looking for eight long years."

"What's your last name, Mandy?"

"Why, it's Kerrigan. You know that, Jack."

"Right. And mine's McConnell. Irish both. It's only the English that have rich relations seeking their lost kin. When the Irish misplace a child, they figure that's just one more potato for all them that's left."

I felt her shiver next to me. "'Tain't fair, Jack."

"Life ain't, mostly."

We were quiet for a time. I almost dozed off.

12

"Jack?"

"Umm?"

"Jack, what're we gonna do about it?"

"How do you mean?"

"We're safe and warm and full now, and have been for probably three days or more. I've lost count. It's been like heaven. But outside it's still winter, and Mr. Huffmaier's got to dig out his bakery sometime."

"So?"

"So we ought to have a plan. Are you going to spend your whole life down here shoveling coal for him?"

"That ain't a fair question, Mandy. You know I ain't had three days like this to think since the diphtheria took my family. I ain't been this full in all that time. Mostly I'm just figuring on how to get something to eat that goes nice with pumpernickel and rye. Or how to keep warm when I leave the bakery. Right now I'm figuring on how to get a new pair of britches and a jacket to go with the other new duds."

"Can I have your old britches when you're through with them?"

"Whyever would you want these old things?"

"I'm tired of skirts. The wind goes right up 'em on most days. I'd ever so much like to be a boy!"

"I dunno, Mandy. If you was a boy, we couldn't be as cozy as this."

"Why not?"

"Not sure, but it wouldn't be seemly, like. And boys, they're always punching at you and things. Then you have to punch back. A fellow can relax more with just a girl around."

Mandy smiled and curled up closer. "Well, maybe I'm glad to be a girl then, for your sake. But I still want your old britches."

"All right. You can have 'em."

Then we slept some more, and never did get around to future plans again.

I suppose it could have been different if I hadn't stuffed myself so for days. Being lean and hungry keeps a body on the alert. But I had stuffed myself, and the sleep came naturally with it, deep and with a peacefulness I'd never known. Fred Huffmaier shoveled through the snow and into the basement door, and still I slept on.

He found me curled up in front of the oven with Mandy. Now a normal person, one who kept religion serious-like, such a normal person might have taken in that innocent sight and maybe even shed a tear of thankfulness and relief that two poor orphans had been spared by the storm. Old Fred had never taken to religion.

His boot hit me in the small of the back first, and I instinctively curled my body tighter around Mandy's, to protect her from the same treatment. For my efforts I received another kick, rougher than the first.

"Sneak thief! Burglar! You stoke my oven at high for five days to keep yourself in comfort! A ton of coal you've cost me! And the eggs you've eaten! You've dared to touch Huffmaier's food! Then you invite your street urchin friends to help eat me out of house and home!"

All this time the blows continued, his feet aided by his fists. A higher, shriller voice joined his from the rear. "I told you time and again no good would come of taking him in like that, Friedreich. Irish trash!"

Mrs. Huffmaier. Couldn't ever mistake her shrewish voice. I felt Mandy's body tremble beneath me, her tears start. I waited for the baker's wrath to lessen. The blows came with less force and he began to cough from the effort.

"Stop, Friedreich. Already you have a cold. Too much exercise will put you in bed with the influenza. These urchins are not worth it. I will go for the police."

"No, Hilda. They are busy digging bodies from the snow."

He was still breathing heavily. I snuck a look from underneath my arms and saw that he was also nursing hands reddened from his assault on me. It was only wishful thinking to hope that he'd broken a few knuckles, or at least strained his kneading muscles.

"He will be sent out into the street. Both of them will."

Mandy and I struggled up. Seeing her tears almost made me forget that every inch of my body ached unmercifully from my beating. But the thought of our good days put new iron in my sagging body, and with fire in my eyes I collected my belongings. I'd miss the warmth and the bread and the *Police Gazette*s, but I sure wouldn't miss Fred Huffmaier.

Mrs. Huffmaier was tapping her booted foot impatiently while I took my time making a bundle of everything I owned in the blanket.

"You let him take these things, Friedreich? You're sure none of them belong to us?"

15

"Enough. I don't need his lice."

Maybe he was beginning to feel a little sorry for what he'd done. He'd certain sure have a time finding another boy who could shovel with such a will as I had. Finally I was packed. I put out my hand to Mandy. "Come on, we'll find a better place."

It was Mrs. Huffmaier who had the last word as we swept out past her. "And see you never set foot in Huffmaier's Bakery again!"

We walked out into a glaring world of ice and snow. And cold. The kind of cold that goes deep down into your very marrow. As the door slammed behind us, I stood and blinked. This was a place I didn't know. We were in an open tunnel, surrounded by mountains of snow. I edged out a few steps. One shoveled tunnel led to others, so many tunnels spreading out into and beyond the street, like the underground burrows of rats suddenly heaved to the surface of the world.

I looked at Mandy. She was still snuffling.

"Dry 'em up, Mandy Kerrigan. Else they'll turn into ice and freeze your face. And pull that muffler up over your head and ears, like mine."

Her gloved hands fumbled with the chore, but couldn't manage it. Exasperated, I put down my bundle and did it for her. "I don't need no baby tagging after me, Mandy. If you want to come along, you'll have to pack it in."

"I was having the most wonderful dream!" And the faucets turned on again. "It was warm and beautiful, springtime. You and I, we were walking together by a stream, or maybe it was bigger, a river. There were flowers and birds singing . . ."

"Mandy, how could you have a dream like that? You ain't never been out of New York City."

"That's why it was so nice. And because you were with me. I wasn't all alone."

I sighed heavily. "All right, then. I'll keep you. But first money we make, we buy some handkerchiefs. Good strong ones. I don't like to see you wiping your nose on your coat like that."

The tears dried up like a flash. "Really, Jack? You'll keep me always with you? Look after me? I can do things for you, too. I can cook if we had a pot and some food. And I can sew. I could fix up that torn jacket of yours, maybe even let down the sleeves. I noticed they have a little hem in them. And I could . . ."

"Stop. I told you it's on, and it's on. Jack McConnell keeps his word. Now let's get out of here. We've got to find a hidey-hole 'fore the sun goes down."

It wasn't as easy as it sounded. I'd gotten a little superior with my sanctuary seemingly guaranteed like that, and hadn't kept up properly with goings-on in the street. My first thought was Flynn's Bakery, soda bread or no.

The mounds of snow made it all that harder to get my bearings and find the way six blocks over. And when we got there I had the day's second disappointment. Another kick, but this one in the gut. I left Mandy and the bundle in the alley behind Flynn's and tunneled through the snow, planning to reconnoiter alone. When I found the chute,

I shimmied through it like it was my own. Only it wasn't. Black Pete Finnigan and his gang had taken over the whole joint. They met me at the bottom of the coal pile, wicked grins on their dirty faces.

"Look who's here!"

"Ain't this German Jack?"

"What's the matter, McConnell? What brings you slumming? Pumpernickel get to you?"

I had my fists up already. It was a sure thing I'd have to defend myself before I got out of this one. Then I felt beyond the gang. Felt, or sensed, 'cause you couldn't see nary a thing in the dark but a few sputtering candles. It ought to have been warm, like Huffmaier's, but it was almost as cold as outside. They'd let the oven die down. But there was something in the air. I sniffed. Cigar smoke. It fairly reeked. The whole lot of 'em had been down here for five days in the cold with nothing to warm them but their tobacco. It was a poor haven at best. They could keep it.

I started backing out, then stumbled on the coal. They were over me in a trice. Fists pummeled at me again, not as hard as Huffmaier's, but just as ferociously. And there were more of them.

It was Mandy that saved me. "Jack! Jack! Coppers coming down the alley! Heading right here!"

Her head was through the chute, yelling like crazy. In less than an instant, Black Pete and his gang were off of me and gone, probably to burrow in the hidden recesses of Flynn's basement, like the vermin they were.

I didn't waste any time myself, but shook off the new pains and climbed the mound of coal to stick my head outside the chute. "Where? Where are they, Mandy?"

She was pulling at me to hurry. "Don't be more of a dolt than you need to, Jack McConnell. Ain't no police, but there'll be more trouble with that gang if we don't clear out fast!"

I felt like hugging her, but settled on a brief look of admiration. Maybe what we had here was more of a partnership, after all. I picked up my bundle and we skedaddled.

Chapter 2

W ELL, WE TRIED three different churches for help, but they was as cold inside as out, and we couldn't be setting up a fire within their walls to warm ourselves. The street markets were useless, too. All the carts were buried under tons of snow. It was getting too fast dark with the coming night and we were in a new neighborhood now, one farther uptown that I wasn't familiar with.

Then I saw the fine town house, sitting strong and firm under its mantle of snow. It had no gaslights on out front, like its neighbors, but its smooth stone walls looked thick and warm against the rising wind. Its windows were shuttered tight, those on the first floor further protected by spiked iron rods.

Now, normally, I wouldn't consider trespassing on something so fine. But this was not a normal situation. We'd been out in the cold for hours and our limbs were growing more sluggish by the minute. Shelter we had to have, and soon, or we'd freeze to death this very night.

There was no hope of entry from the front. It was too

public. I cajoled Mandy into keeping a stiff upper lip for just a little longer and led her around to the back. I cleared off the area in the alley where the coal chute ought to be. No help there. It was bolted with an iron padlock. But there was one spot where the winds had drifted the snow to just above the top of the first-floor windows. If the drift had iced over enough, there was just the chance I could climb it and break into the second floor. Mandy saw the look on my face as these considerations were cogitating. I swear, that girl could read minds.

"You won't go sinking into that drift and be gone from me forever, will you, Jack?"

"It weren't my intention."

"Do it quickly, then, while you still have the strength."

"It ain't against your morals?"

"Beating people is against my morals, and stealing from those who are kind. Cold churches are against my morals, too. Finding shelter in an empty house ain't."

I nodded in agreement. "Now we got our operatin' principles sorted out, I guess I can tackle this here mountain."

I rummaged through my bundle for the shoeshine kit. The hardest object I could think of was my polishing brush. I didn't no way intend to crash through that window with my bare fists. Neither did I intend to tear up my new leather gloves. Finally armed, I began the ascent. There was a good, crisp outer coating of ice over the drift. My boots sank into it once or twice, but not more than a foot. At last I was before the window. It was shuttered tight, and from the inside, but I pulled my glove off with my teeth and managed to slip my fingers through the narrow opening and jog at the clasp. It was frozen, and my feet were beginning to slip. I floundered for a better footing, hanging on to the shutters. Just as my legs flew out behind me into empty air, the right-hand shutter came loose in my hand with a groan, then stood creaking by one hinge. But it was enough.

Hanging on for dear life with one hand, I groped in my pocket for the brush. There it was. I didn't have too many chances left, swinging up there. Summoning up any hidden, unfrozen resources, I gave that window a thunderous whack. The shards flew inwards with my hand, and my head soon followed. In a moment, it was done. I was inside.

I took a moment to knock out a bit more glass, so's Mandy wouldn't get too cut up, then I slithered down the pile for her and the bundle. I got Mandy up first, mostly pushing and lifting from behind, then went back for the bundle. That was worse. The snowdrift was becoming as slick as a toboggan run. I huffed, puffed, slipped, and finally made it to Mandy's outstretched arms. I was in again.

Mandy gave me a hug, and we did a little dance for sheer joy. Then I took a final look out the window.

"Anybody walking up this alley, a copper for instance, could figure out, clear as day, what we done, Mandy. We got to cover our trail."

"Won't the wind do it? It's starting to sling bits of snow and ice around again."

"Like as not, that'll take too long." I opened the bundle

and let the contents scatter. Hanging out the window, I swung that blanket as far down as possible, so our footprints slurred together, till it looked like maybe just some children had been playing there. Then I reached for the broken shutter and managed to latch it together again. I turned around to find that our refuge had become pitch dark.

"Didn't you pack that last candle, Jack?"

"Good girl. I did, indeed." After some groping, the candle and my matchbox were found. There was a satisfying stroke of the match against the floorboards, then light.

"Ooh. Jack, I ain't never been in a place like this."

Neither had I. The flickering candle revealed bits of a grand room. High ceilings, maybe twelve foot; fancy geegaws all over the plasterwork. And a fireplace. For the rest, it was quite empty, except for a lovely angel painted on the ceiling, surrounded by puffy white clouds. I held the candle as high as I could so we could better admire her. Then my arm got tired.

"Let's check out some more."

Mandy didn't want to leave that angel, but I pulled her from room to empty room, admiring other painted ceilings, polished floors, but nothing else. I kept looking for something we could burn in one of those fireplaces. We walked until we found a staircase, then followed it down two flights. In the basement we found it. A still full coal room next to the kitchen. Guess the owners hadn't figured it was worth their time to clean that out as well. Enough coal was lying there to last us through the winter. I stood there gaping at it, until Mandy lost patience and pulled the candle from my hand.

"Hey! I can't see!"

She was in the kitchen again. "They've left the coal bucket and shovel, and a big old cooking pot, Jack." She wandered back, pleased as punch. "Let's live in the room upstairs, the one with the clouds and angel on the ceiling."

"But it's got glass on the floor from where we broke in. And there'll be a draft—"

"We can fix it, Jack. Please?"

I smiled through the darkness. "If you want it that bad, you shall have it."

It took the end papers from *Oliver Twist* to get a bit of coal going. I was feeling stubborn. If that didn't work, I'd have frozen before going into the first chapters. But it wasn't necessary. We built the fire carefully and in half an hour had a warm glow and heat.

I was feeling hungry and sleepy, but Mandy took the stub of our last candle and went off to explore some more. She surely was enjoying our new home.

I fixed up our bed in front of the coals and was just spreading myself out when I heard a strange noise, sort of a wet, gasping sound, followed by a little scream. I bolted up and ran out of the room into the hall, almost bashing myself into the far wall in the dark.

"Mandy! You all right?"

I found her in a small closet two doors down. She was standing and staring in awe as she pulled a long cord that seemed to be dangling from the ceiling. I heard that same gasping sound again.

"Whatever is it, Jack?"

I looked over the flickering candle and couldn't help but roar. "It's a water closet, Mandy!"

"What's it for?"

"Why, it's an indoor privy."

"Ooh."

"And they got a sink, too."

I turned a gilded knob experimentally. Water flowed out. Handy, that. "We landed ourselves good and proper this time, Mandy. Don't even have to pump for our water."

She looked over the sink admiringly. "And here I was fixing to lean out the window for some snow to melt in our pot. Oh, Jack! This is ever so lovely!"

She gave me a hug, and then the candle gave out.

"That'd be sufficient excitement for this day. Bedtime, girl."

We groped our way back to the fire.

My empty stomach woke me up. A pale, weak light struggled through the shutters of our room. I threw some more coal on the dying fire, then sat warming myself until Mandy stretched and sat up.

"I'm hungry."

"Me, too."

"What shall we do?"

"I guess we'd better find some boots to black."

We couldn't use the bolted coal chute, so finally settled on the servants' rear entrance. In the daylight we could see that the owners had obligingly left the key dangling from a nail next to the lock. I searched in my pockets for a bit of string to hang it from, then pulled it over my head. I'd never owned a key before. I didn't intend to lose this one, either. It felt good, like I'd come up in the world.

But I didn't stay up there too long. Business was rotten. With all the snow starting to melt everywhere, people didn't seem inclined to polish up boots that would get muddied again in minutes. If only I'd had Huffmaier's shovel, I could have made my fortune. We wandered around for hours and finally only had eighteen cents to show for it. It was still cold and I was hungrier than ever. Huffmaier's day-old bread would've tasted good right then.

I took the few coins out of my pocket and stared at them disconsolately.

Mandy was staring, too. "Jack, we've got enough now."

"How you figure that?"

"We can get a beef bone for that, and some carrots and potatoes, maybe even an onion. I can make us some soup."

"You know how, truly? You weren't just joshing with me?"

"I wouldn't do that, Jack. I've been cooking for my pa forever, seems like."

We hunted up a greengrocer's first, then she went and spent all the money on vegetables and a twist of salt. I was fuming as we walked out.

"Where you figure on getting that soup bone now?"

"If I can't buy it, I'll beg it."

And she did. It took three separate butchers to do it,

but she came out of the last one with a smile of triumph and a newspaper-wrapped bundle.

"Me being hungry didn't help with the first two, so I told this one I'd a great dog that was teething. He wrapped me up some bones right away for it. There's even a little meat on them!"

That pot of soup lasted us near a week as the snow melted and we slowly got back on our feet. We were selling papers now, both of us on opposite street corners, Mandy the *Times* and me the *Tribune*, just to hedge our bets. I'd had to give her some lessons on the way of it, though. Like some days there just didn't seem to be any news worth crying out. I mean, if I'd the three cents to buy a paper, I sure wouldn't have bothered. But like I said earlier, I been around the streets a while. Times like this is when a smart newsboy had to make his own news. I had me some good headlines saved up for such occasions.

One particularly dull day, Mandy and I had stood there it seemed for hours without selling but half a dozen out of our stock. There wouldn't be any hot dinner at this rate. I gave Mandy a high sign across the street, between the splashing carriages and omnibuses. She knew what it meant. "Spark up and pay attention!" A fresh mob of businessmen come down the street.

"Extra! Extra! New edition hot off the press! Queen Victoria kicks the bucket!"

"What's that, young man?" A nickel was thrust at me and a paper grabbed. The score didn't even wait for his change.

"Extra! Extra! Empire in mourning!"

Well, my pile went mighty fast, then I deemed it appropriate to make tracks before I was discovered. Coins jingling in my pocket, I sauntered across the street to Mandy. "What's the matter, girl? Your pile's most as high as before!"

"I heard what you said. How could you, Jack?"

"How could I what?"

"Call somebody dead like that? Specially the Queen of England?"

"I was just precipitatin' the event a little. Can't expect her to live forever, can you? No one does."

" 'Tain't right. It's dishonest. And here I was standing next to a little old man who had tears in his eyes when he heard what you said. He even bought one of my papers, and when he couldn't find anything about the Queen, I had to lie and say I probably had an earlier edition than you. Well, I'm just not going to sell papers anymore if you ever do that again."

That had me stumped. I never expected such a fuss over a little thing like using some originality. And here we were stuck with all these dull copies of the *Times*. I picked one up and gave the front page a good going-over. There had to something there. It took me a while, but I finally found it.

I looked at Mandy. "Is it all right with you to expand on what really is in the paper?"

"Long as it's there. See—" She pointed to the little box up at the top. "It says 'All the news that's fit to print.' They wouldn't go putting lies in there."

"Sez you," I muttered to myself. But I'd found the small

headline that read "Rome Approves Fraternal Organization" and shouted out, "Extra! Extra! Pope says no excommunication for Knights of Columbus!" Well, after a few minutes, that got some response from the Irishmen drinking in the saloon behind us. I never could see what the Church had against brotherly organizations anyhow. And it did get the papers sold.

Our life got to take on a certain pattern. We'd start out with some soup for breakfast, then work the papers through the first three or four editions. Then we'd leave off and go into our bootblacking routine till dark. We had a stock of oatmeal for porridge now, two real tins for sugar and salt, a little kerosene lamp to see by, and handkerchiefs for both of us. Mandy saw to that. Pulled me right up by the bootstraps on my promise, she did.

We also stocked in some soap and a length of rope. Mandy had found a working tub in another of those closets and had insisted we bathe—and even wash our clothes —come Sundays. I wasn't too keen on waltzing around that big old house all the first Sunday in my blanket while my duds dried, but she would have it her way. She said we'd have to start saving up for a second set of underwear and shirts for each of us, too. It seemed excessive to me, but I didn't have too much to say in the matter.

January kind of melted into February. We'd got real comfortable in our mansion. We owned a set of spoons, cups, and bowls now, not to mention a fry pan and a coffeepot. It was a sheer pleasure after a hard day at work to sneak back into our house, cook a hot meal, and lounge under that guardian angel. Even the hardness of the polished floor didn't set my back off anymore.

We had a pile of free newspapers to read through, and then we had our "dream" book. This was a kind of combination geography and atlas I'd spied at a bookseller's and couldn't get out of my mind. When we finally had the price for a new shirt, I just took the money and bought the book instead. Mandy didn't mind too much after she started looking into it. We'd sit there at night looking at maps and pictures of places we'd never get to, dreaming about them and how they had to be better than New York City. It was mostly in our heads, I guess. We could of took to the rails like hoboes I'd heard tell of, but wasn't anything going to take us from our mansion right then. I guess we figured we'd just live there forever, with nobody to account for save ourselves. A month went by and we clean forgot that anybody owned the place but us.

It was a morning in late February. A Monday morning. I knew, 'cause my freshly washed shirt was still hanging by the fire. What woke me was a terrible commotion one floor below, by the front door. I pulled on that shirt, shoved Mandy awake, and raced to the top of the big stairs, then stood staring, half hid behind the wooden banisters, heart dropping, at the sight before me.

"What is it?" She was cowering behind me now, her hair all askew, and still rubbing sleep out of her eyes.

"Eviction day. That's furniture coming in the front door."

Mandy stared at me for a moment in terror, then we both raced back to our room and started slinging our pack

together again. It took longer than I'd have liked. We'd
collected more than seemed possible in a short month,
more than we could sneak out with, quietly-like. I sure
did hate to leave the pots and lamp and those tins of food.
But then we were dressed and creeping down the back
stairs and out the delivery door. I kept the key. Maybe
it would fit another house someday. A permanent one.

It was raining, worse luck. I didn't feel like selling
papers. We just shifted miserably around that big city,
darting in and out of awnings and overhangs, filling up
on weak one-cent coffee at the pavement shacks. And it
kept raining. We finally settled for the night in a filthy
tenement hallway. We'd had to pay three cents apiece for
the privilege of a lying space from the fellow who'd rented
rights from the landlord, and huddled together beneath
the stink of our wet wool blanket. We'd come down some
in the world, but hardly noticed. The heart was all taken
out of us.

Chapter 3

"ONE MOMENT, Mr. Simmons. What about these two?"

I shifted open an eye and stared from under a frayed corner of the blanket warily. Was it morning already? Then there was a boot prodding at me, curious-like.

"You there. Are you awake? Alive?"

It was a lady and a man. The lady had an hourglass shape like posters I'd seen of Miss Lillian Russell outside Tony Pastor's Theatre in the Bowery, only more stuffed, but her face wasn't near so pretty, or young. The man was skinny, with a pinched, sour look. His black suit hung loose on his frame, and his eyes had the burning look I'd seen in some preachers. Trouble, here we come again.

The blanket was lifted from my head tentatively, with gloved fingers.

"Don't get too close now, Miss Gertrude. One never can tell what kind of diseases street urchins carry."

"Thank you for the timely reminder, Mr. Simmons."

She was looking straight into my eyes now. "Up, young man. And you may awaken that other bundle as well."

I nudged Mandy. "Visitors, girl. High-toned, uptown ones."

Mandy opened her eyes, took one look, and cringed behind me.

"Come now, we haven't all day. Do you wish to be saved or not?"

We shambled to our feet. Wasn't sure about Mandy, but all that wet yesterday hadn't done no favors to my body. I sneezed, then reached for my handkerchief to mop up the results. Our audience stepped back out of the way of further assaults.

"What you have in mind to save us from, and what've we gotta do for it?"

"I'll thank you to take a better tone when speaking to your superiors, young man."

I gave the fellow in black the eye, then turned my defiant glare at the lady.

"Rough, Mr. Simmons, no doubt about it. But he does own a handkerchief. Perhaps he has redeeming qualities."

"No one has yet taught him the proper sequence in using such a tool, I fear."

That Simmons, he was still staying a wary distance from my germs.

"If you're planning on palavering all day about my handkerchief, we'll just excuse ourselves." I turned to Mandy behind me. "Come on, we got breakfast to find."

I ignored them both and began to pick up the belongings we'd used as pillows so's they wouldn't get stolen in the night. A sharp pain stabbed into my ear as I was grabbed by the lobe and slowly pulled up. Simmons had a mean streak hiding beneath that frail exterior. But before I could say anything about it, Mandy went and bit his hand. It must have been hard, 'cause he let go of my ear fast.

"Criminal element, Miss Gertrude, both of them. I think it's time we moved on and left them to their own devices."

"No. Wait. All the more reason to get them off the streets now, before they become further hardened. Never let it be said that members of the Children's Aid Society shirked in their duties."

I had my belongings together now. Children's Aid Society, my foot. They could as easily be slavers. I was ready to dodge out soon's I could give Mandy the look. Miss Gertrude squelched it. My ma never shoulda tried to instill manners in me. When that lady started in again, I just stood there like a dummy, answering her questions.

"What is your name, young man?"

"Jack McConnell."

"Your age?"

"Near enough to eleven."

"Your residence?"

"Wherever I lay my head."

"And you, miss?"

I near fainted when Mandy bobbed a little curtsy before answering. "Amanda Kerrigan. I'm eight, and I live where Jack does."

Miss Gertrude beamed at Simmons. "You see? It just takes the correct tone." She turned to us again. "Come along. You're going with us on a trip."

"Where?"

"On a lovely train ride, out West. You are about to be given the opportunity of a lifetime, deserving or not. When

34

the Society gets finished cleaning you up, even Lady Astor will be proud of you."

Mandy and I, we were summarily marched out of that tenement into another dank gray morning. Inwardly I was shaking. We'd been caught by the do-gooders, or worse. God help us now.

We were hustled into a wagon filled with other unfortunates like us. Mandy and I stood by the rear opening, watching the Bend of Mulberry Street and Five Points disappear behind us. Soon we were through Chinatown with its laundries and opium dens and out of the East Side completely, making our way up Broadway.

At Thirtieth Street the wagon stopped and all the girls were hustled out and into a brownstone lodging house. Mandy cried and hung on to me fiercely, so's they had to pull her away with some force. Before she finally let go, I whispered into her ear: "Don't fret, girl. I'll come get you soon's I can."

And I would, too. Only this time I'd come prepared. I was kicking myself good and hard then for never getting that second pair of britches. If I had, Mandy could of been in them, and passing for a boy. They wouldn't of separated us then.

Well, I didn't have to wonder much longer where I was being taken. The wagon stopped a few blocks farther north, at Thirty-fifth Street, in front of another brownstone. It looked a little like the one we'd taken shelter in before our eviction, but the insides were a world different.

They herded me and the other boys out, not touching us, like we was diseased nags bound for the glue factory, then run us through the worst the establishment had to offer. I won't bore you with details, but them foot baths and delousing and all the rest of it weren't no fun. Neither was the questions they asked whilst society ladies wrote down the answers on big forms as we took our turns standing before them.

Now, I don't mean to say that all these ladies was heartless, like that Miss Gertrude seemed. Some of them appeared to truly care. You could tell when they smiled at you. One of them, a Miss Blackman, had smiles to spare for all the boys, seemed like. And even a few hugs. I got one of them and like to never let go, she smelled so good. Even her masses of blond hair had the scent of lavender. But she was just helping out, searching for the right-size duds, and didn't really seem to have no say in the main business.

Least I got a new pair of britches in the clothing line, longer ones. They tried to put me in knickerbockers, and I kicked up a storm till Miss Blackman agreed I was old enough for real pants. The good thing, aside from the new britches, was that I'd seen the storeroom where they kept the clean duds. It wouldn't be nothing to nip in there and grab a set of clothes for Mandy when the time was ripe. And the way they was pushing and polishing us, looked like that would be mighty soon.

Well, I was taking in my new quarters all the time this was going on. It wasn't really much cleaner than tenements I'd slept in before, just smelled worse from that stuff do-gooders slop all over such places—like the hospital my family'd been carted off to—trying to make people think they're clean. A nasty smell, that. The wall paint was peeling, and the towels slung over the cleaning troughs was almost black. Everything was done by troughs, seemed like—washing, eating, even sleeping—tho' I gotta admit the beds weren't that bad. Sheets and everything they had. That part was better than the sleeping boards at the Police Station Lodging House down in the Bend. Even better than the strips of canvas strung between rough timbers all in a row at the seven-cents-a-night places. But it wasn't better than my freedom, no sir.

Didn't see anything more of Simmons and Miss Gertrude, either, least not then. They must have been just procurers. For I'd pretty much figured out this scam to my mind. The Children's Aid Society was only a front. What we'd got mixed up with was a bunch of slavers, like I'd originally suspicioned, all except for that Miss Blackman, who mustn't have understood the Society's true purpose either. Even my mama had known about the slavers. She'd always have me keep a good eye out for my little sister Becky when we was out on the street. Said she didn't nohow want us near Chinatown, for one thing. Little children just got gobbled up and disappeared there. And these people were after our bodies. They even had a doctor examine us, testing muscle strength and the like. Being a boy, I figured the white slavers wouldn't want me, but I feared mightily for Mandy. What'd they plan on using us for, onct we got out West?

I got into some conversations with a few of the other fellows on this subject. One, about my age, called Zeb, guessed they was just gonna ship us out as hard labor for the planting and harvesting season.

"They got a body shortage out there on them Great

Plains. Since they chased off the Injuns an' all. Stands to reason. I reckon they're gonna work us worse than the sweats, then come winter either send us back here to starve or just set us loose. We'll probably freeze to death in them great snowstorms."

"Worse than what we had here last month?"

"Course. Snow comes down ever so high. Twict as tall as a tenement house."

We was sitting at a long table, stuffing on hot porridge and tea. Every so often, Zeb, he'd pinch up a lump of that unsweetened porridge and kind of offhandedly move it under the table. Well, this got up my natural curiosity after a while.

"I know this grub ain't great, but what you throwing it on the floor for?"

"Sssh. Ain't going on no floor. It's for my buddies."

I squinched closer and looked down at his lap. Underneath the tablecloth was two of the niftiest mice I ever did see. They was up on their hind legs, laying into their dinners.

"The white one is Tit, t'other gray one Tat. They been everywhere with me more'n a year now."

"Society gonna let you take 'em West?"

"Ain't gonna ask. Just gonna do it. Tit an' Tat, they're my only family. Don't see how I could manage without 'em."

My admiration was great. I could see right off the benefits of such a family. Instant company without the strains brought on by humans. Still, that scene, it brought Mandy's face before me again in an instant.

"I got a family, too. A 'dopted sister."

"That girl I saw you with in the wagon?"

I nodded assent.

"She sure did carry on some when they took her from you."

"Don't worry. I'm gonna get her back."

"I know what you mean. A fellow needs somebody."

Well, then a bell was rung and we was hustled off to the beds. Zeb tucked those mice into his pockets real casual-like, and nobody ever knew they was there. It was a pity Mandy was too big for my pocket.

I slept hard after all the stresses of that day, and got through the next few days all right, mostly biding my time and eating everything I got my hands on. They give us a few classes to see if we could read and such, but there was a lot of time left over for the fellows to play poker or seven-eleven and shoot craps in the corners. I don't take to gambling as a rule, but times was slow and I had a few pennies left from before they caught me, so I pitched in. I had a winning streak and raised my pot to fifteen cents before I went and lost it all. I guess I got kind of mad when that happened and was about to lose my temper when Miss Blackman walked over out of nowhere. Three sets of hands that had been readying themselves to stave off my fists dropped.

"Why, Jack, have you been gambling?"

I ducked my head down, shifted my feet, and mumbled.

She stooped down before me and lifted my chin so's I could see into her eyes. "You lost everything, didn't you?"

"Yes, ma'am."

"How does that make you feel?"

"Like kicking myself for the fool I am."

"A fool for playing, or a fool for losing?"

"Why, for losing, ma'am. If I'd a won, would have been all right, wouldn't it?"

She shook her head sadly, but there was a twinkle in her eye. "Nothing in this life comes easy, Jack. If you gamble away your talents, you'll soon find you've nothing left."

"Aw, I can make up that fifteen cents in an hour on the street. In good weather."

"It wasn't the fifteen cents I was referring to, young man. And I think you know that." She was still stooped down and her voice went into a private whisper as she took my chin in her hand and looked me in the eye. "You've got something in you I don't see in many of the others. When you leave us here, try to make the most of it."

Well, by this time we'd worked up a little audience and I was getting kind of embarrassed, so I just sort of edged away with a "Thank you, ma'am," and ran off to find Zeb and his mice.

That Miss Blackman always seemed to be keeping one eye on me after that episode. It didn't give me much room to get into any more mischief, but it did start me thinking that maybe she might be an inside friend. When I got comfortable with that idea, I got up the courage to ask about my kit that the Society had mostly gobbled up with my old clothes. So I sidled up to her in between meals and put the question to her.

"Ma'am?"

"Yes, Jack?"

"Are they planning on giving me back my kit when we head out of here?"

"If you mean those horrid old clothes that the ragman wouldn't even take, no. You'll not be needing them in Nebraska."

"It ain't them I was referring to, ma'am. It was my books."

One eyebrow went up. "Books?"

"Yes, ma'am. My Dickens and my dream book—a sort of geography, that was."

"Charles Dickens?"

"Yes, ma'am! I admire him greatly. Only read the one so far, though, on account of I ain't been near to enough spending money to buy more." I stopped, an upsetting thought beginning to nag at me. "You suppose they got booksellers out West? And a way to make some spending money for the buying?"

She laughed. "I believe a fair amount of the Western population is literate, Jack. And yes, they ought to have books, too." Then she turned serious. "But if you came with books, they never should have been parted from you. Heaven knows it's a rare enough occurrence among the Society's inmates. Let me look into it for you."

"Thank you, ma'am. I'm mighty attached to them."

And so I wandered off, but not before catching a curious look in Miss Blackman's eyes as they followed me out of the room.

So the time passed, and I got to feeling lazy and full up in the stomach again. But in the middle of the fourth night

I bolted up dead awake. I just listened to the darkness for a while, and the all-over breathing sounds. Then I heard a church bell somewhere near strike three. Something told me it was time to fetch Mandy. I picked up my new clothes and my blacking box. It was the only thing they'd let me keep. I'd managed to stuff my jackknife and my matchbox into it, too, before those disappeared as well. Then I tiptoed out of that big room, right past the cubicle where the matron slept.

Out in the hallway I got dressed in everything but my good boots, then slipped down the stairs to the storeroom. It wasn't even locked, though I could of dealt with an easy one like that if necessary. I struck a match against the darkness and pulled down a set of clothes for Mandy and jackets for both of us. I figured it wasn't stealing, only a fair exchange for my old clothes and blanket, and the books the Society people had taken from me. Miss Blackman hadn't gotten back to me on the book subject yet, so I guessed they was gone forever. It hurt, like losing good friends, but there wasn't much I could do about it now. I pulled on my boots and was gone.

The stars were out. I took that as a good sign and passed the five blocks whistling beneath my breath. I got my first setback at the front door to the girls' home. It was closed up solid tight. I had to go around to the back. That was bolted, too, but they'd clean forgotten about the coal chute. I tucked all our supplies behind an ash barrel and did what came natural to me. It weren't no time at all before I was in my stocking feet on the second floor, searching in a big dormitory room, bed by bed, for Mandy.

She jumped when I touched her, but didn't say nothing.

She just slid out of that bed and followed me, boots in hand, trusting as ever. I didn't even let her talk after she'd been dressed in the back alley. I wasn't taking no more chances at this point. It wasn't till we were sitting on a dock by the East River, shivering and watching the sun rise, that I let up.

"How you like them pants, Mandy?"

She hugged her legs together with her arms. "Ever so nice, Jack. They're much warmer than skirts."

"Good." I thought for a good bit more while the sun crept slowly higher and higher, glittering now on the garbage bobbing down the river. "I figure you gotta play at being a boy for a while, Mandy. So if they catch us again, we won't be separated like last time."

She was nibbling the edges of the braid they'd done her hair up in, considering. "What about this?"

"Only boys I know got braids live in Chinatown."

She thought over that for a while, then, "Still got your jackknife?"

"You bet."

"Then fetch it out and cut my hair, Jack."

"You sure?" Suddenly it was me getting cold feet. She looked mighty cute with her hair done up like that. "We could maybe find you a hat and tuck the braid under it."

"I'm sure as sure. They always keep the girls from the boys, Jack. We learned that in the wagon." And she held up that braid to me like it was some kind of sacrificial offering.

"Well—all right, then." I dug out my knife and slowly hacked through the braid at the top, till the whole thing came off. Mandy sat and held that braid in her lap for a while. Then, before I could stop her, she just pitched it off the dock into the river. We watched it float down the current and disappear.

"Can you tidy the rest of it up, like yours? I want ever so much to look like a real boy." She was getting excited about the idea. "Just think, Jack, now I can go everywhere with you! I can run as fast as I want, without those old skirts stopping me, and I can learn to cuss and smoke cigar butts—"

"No, indeed! I won't have you cussing or smoking no butts. I've given up on both myself. Won't have your growth stunted thataways."

She put on a pout. "No fair, Jack. You're trying to take the fun out of it all!"

"Well, then, just to keep the fun in, next time we get into a fight, I'll let you defend yourself with your very own fists."

"Really? You will? Maybe you'd better be giving me a few lessons, just in case."

I sighed. That was supposed to have discouraged her some, but it only seemed to have added icing to the cake.

"We'll see." And I went at her head again. Soon she had a convincing ragged look. A barber could have done better, but I didn't know any that handed out free cuts, like me. I gave her the once-over while I snapped my knife shut and tucked it into the nearest pocket. Her face still had that open, girlish look. And those eyelashes. But then, I'd seen young boys with that same look before. She'd do.

We sat some more, comfortable just being back together, till we figured it was late enough in the morning to look for work.

I guess I could of got credit for some papers on Newspaper Row, but I figured that's where the Society people would look first, if they was interested enough in trying to pursue us. So we took, instead, to walking north, stopping every so often to set up shop and black a few boots. Business wasn't bad, and before you knew it, we had enough for a good meal. Then we kept walking farther north. It hardly ever occurred to me before, but there was other parts to the city aside from the East Side and its tenement world we were used to. I guess a body just sticks around places where it seems to belong most comfortably.

We kept on hiking clear into Central Park. Mandy stopped as the trees and fields of winter-yellowed grass spread before us. "Is this the country, Jack?"

"You never been in Central Park before?"

"Never!"

Her eyes were big with the wonder of the open spaces. There wasn't nothing for it but to keep going some more till we got to the sheep meadow. She'd never seen sheep, either.

At the first sight she grabbed me hard and just stared. "What are they?" It was a whisper of awe.

"Sheep."

"They're so gentle and soft-looking! My, but I'd love to touch one!" She turned and flapped those eyes at me a few times. They still worked, even with the haircut.

I never knew sheep was so skittish. We chased them

clear across the meadow and up to the edge of the frozen lake, where I finally got my hands on what looked to be a newborn lamb, slower than the others. It was shivering in my arms and Mandy was reaching out fingers to touch it when something give me a jolt like I never felt before.

"What in thunder . . . !"

I must have been butted through the air six feet by that baby's mama, and Mandy, she was lying on the ground laughing her fool head off, till I picked myself up to find the flock clean gone.

"Ain't funny." I was rubbing where it hurt. Took me right back to my pa's occasional whalings. But his razor strap never did have that kind of a kick.

"Oh, but it was, Jack! You couldn't see that mama's face. She knew just what she was doing!" Then she was sober again, wiping tears of laughter from her face. "You suppose they've got human mamas like that? Ones who would kill for their offspring?"

I was on my feet again. "I reckon mine would have, all right. Only she never got the chance."

And then I noticed it had almost gone dark on us, while we'd been frittering away the afternoon chasing livestock. "I hope you ain't as hungry as I am, Mandy, 'cause we're nowhere near food, and we've got to find us lodgings for the night."

"Do we have to leave here? Couldn't the park be our home? It's almost as nice as our old house, only not as warm."

"You're right there." I looked around desperately. "Let's explore those boats. Maybe they'll do for the night."

"Wouldn't it be wonderful to just fall asleep in a boat with the water kind of rocking you around?"

I gave her an eye. The novelty of the park was still making her silly, that was sure. "They're all froze solid. Besides, there ain't no waves in a pond anyhow."

"Why, Jack, don't you know how to dream?"

"I ain't got time for make-believing, Mandy. Empty stomachs don't get full up on fairy tales."

She sighed like she knowed I was right but wished it weren't so anyhow. Then I gave her a little shove to get her back to the present business and we kind of slid over the edge of the ice at the shallows, because it was softening up in the center. It was just as well. If it'd still been good and hard, there wouldn't be any peace or shelter for us here. The whole place would be crowded with the gentry skating. It must be nice to have that kind of energy left at the end of the day.

We pulled open and snuck under the canvas cover of a boat that had been left to freeze right there. Curled up in its damp bottom, I was missing the rest of our kit most desperately. The blanket, and even more our two books.

I woke inside what felt like a cold, airless tomb. I struggled away from Mandy's warmth and prodded up at the canvas cover. It didn't want to give. I positioned my head and shoulders under the end piece, where we'd come in, and tried it again. This time I was rewarded with about a foot of powdery snow all over my head.

"Tarnation!"

That woke Mandy up. "What is it now, Jack?"

"It went and snowed again last night, that's all."

The sight of me looking like a snowman should have cheered her up, but it didn't. She inched over and stuck her head out as well. It was still coming down.

"Oh, Jack!" It was a wail. "It never before in my life snowed and rained like it has since I ran away from my pa!"

"That's 'cause you never had need to take notice of the weather before. You were all warm in your room, just looking out."

"That isn't so! For one thing, we were always short on coal. For another, I had to go out first thing every day with the growler, down to the saloon to fetch pa's morning beer. And that beer can always seemed heavier in the cold."

"Yep, I done enough of that in my time, too. Least the saloons was always warm, warmer than our rooms. It got so us kids had to be kicked home by the bartender for cluttering up drinking space."

"But if you slipped on ice or a crack or something and spilled any of it coming home, then there was the walloping to look forward to." She was off and running now. "Even in fine weather, if you took too much time to get back and the suds had died down so it didn't look like so much in the growler, why, pa'd beat me then, too. He said I was drinking it myself. And I wouldn't ever! It's nasty stuff!"

I ducked my head back under the shelter of the canvas again. "I don't know. Even beer might look good right now. My stomach is acting up something terrible."

She felt for her own. "Mine, too. Worse than when we

ate only once a day before. Do you suppose it was all that food at the Society?"

"Probably their way of subvertin' us. Get us used to three squares a day, so's we'd never want to leave."

Mandy's face had taken on a dreamy look now in the weak light filtering in through the front of the boat. "I don't know but it was that bad, Jack. The ladies didn't yell too much, and nobody beat me. And they was the cleanest, softest beds I ever did sleep in."

"Come on, Mandy, you want to go back? Is that what you're saying?"

"The only thing I missed was you, Jack. If I had you with me, I'd take my chances with the Society and their journey in a minute."

"What about our freedom, then? You want to be accountable to grownups for the rest of your life? Ordering you about, feeding you worse than on the street, beating you whenever they like?"

"They didn't feed us worse than on the street. You said so yourself."

"Well, there was plenty to eat, right enough, even if it weren't fancy. But that's not my main point. My main point is the rest, or maybe just the accountable part." I had to stop and scratch my head now, to give me some time to think. This here was more trickerous to work out than I'd thought.

But Mandy, she just goes breezing on. "You said your mother wasn't like that."

"Don't you go bringing my ma into this. She's not what I was referring to. Besides, she's for sure a saint in heaven now."

Mandy ignored this last and crawled over me to look out at the snow again. "All I can say is, it's a pretty poor freedom we have right now, Jack. No fire, no breakfast, no blankets."

All that running of fingers through my hair in frustration just made cold snow slide down my neck, setting goose bumps down my back. "We'll get set up again, Mandy! A few good days on the street and we can buy ourselves another blanket. Maybe even some more mufflers." I was getting desperate now. I didn't like the way this talk was heading.

"And find another house, Jack? And be evicted again? Have our things taken again, like the Society people did? How many times do we have to do that?"

I tried to give her a rough hug, but she slipped out of my grasp. "It'll be better soon. It's almost spring! And summers, why, summers are a breeze to get through. There's nothing so nice as sleeping under the stars on a hot night."

I knew she could be stubborn, but I'd never seen that particular look on her face before. "Jack McConnell! Look outside again. Please! We've got two, maybe three months of cold coming yet. And I'm hungry!"

Then she turned on the tears. It made me desperate, those tears did.

"All right, then! We'll go back! But this time you'll come with me. And if things don't turn out right in the West, don't you never tell me about it!"

She pulled out her handkerchief and had a good blow. But she didn't hide her eyes fast enough to keep a kind of sly look of victory out of them. She knew what she'd pulled and won all right.

I mumbled some to myself about how on earth I ever got roped down by this female anyhow. Me, Jack McConnell, a free-born American male who'd been looking after himself just fine before she turned up. But in my heart I knew why it had all come about. Even free-born American males needed somebody to call their own. And in a funny way Mandy suited me.

So we pulled ourselves out of that boat and headed south again out of the park. I didn't wait for Mandy to catch up with me, but walked fast as I could, her trailing a few yards behind. We'd nearly made it back to Columbus Circle and Broadway when she finally put on a burst of speed and grabbed my arm, huffing and puffing.

"Don't be mad at me, please?"

I ignored her, but slowed up a little. A few more blocks south and I'd worked off most of my spleen. Then I started in telling her about Zeb and his mice, and Miss Blackman. Miss Blackman I described in glorious detail: her hair like the sun, her blue eyes, even the line of her jaw that showed she owned a little character. Mandy, bless her, wanted to know what kind of dresses she wore.

"Blue," I said. "Blue like her eyes, with just enough lace to show she's a true lady."

By the time we got to Thirty-fifth Street, we were friends again.

I knocked at the big door with not a little trepidation in my heart. It was justified. Mr. Simmons opened it. He stared at my snow-covered self for a few seconds until recognition dawned.

"Well, well. What have we here? Might this be the prodigal's return?"

I didn't know nothing about any prodigals, but a quick chill went through me as I realized he might spot out Mandy right off. Then the game would be up for sure.

"Please, sir, I had to fetch my orphan cousin. He ain't got nobody else in the world, and if I just took off and disappeared on him, he might die. He's littler, see, and not as strong."

I turned to Mandy, who was shivering quite authentically behind me. She'd caught on to the game, though, and had her chin and most of her face hunched into her coat. She looked pitiful for sure.

My head swiveled back to Simmons. "Ain't nothing a spell out West won't cure, sir."

"You're too late for redemption, both of you."

I could feel my heart freeze still. "Beg pardon, sir. How's that?"

"Your timing was off by a day, young man. The orphan train left New York this morning."

"But Miss Blackman—"

"Miss Blackman journeyed with it."

The scream of frustration I felt building inside was forced back as a plump, matronly woman huffed up behind Simmons and lashed into him like she was the boss.

"Sure now, Mr. Simmons, you're always the one to complain about the coal bill. And here you be with the front door open to the winter! Are you fixing to let it all in?"

There she stood like rock, arms astride her ample hips, glaring.

He stiffly turned to acknowledge her presence. "Back to the kitchen with you, Cook. It's just a few street arabs too late for the train."

She bustled past his figure to bend down to us. "And you'd send them back into the snow? For shame, Mr. Simmons! And we've this great empty house to heat for no one but the two of us? Come back to the kitchen with me this minute, the both of you. I've naught to do before going off to visit my grandchildren tomorrow anyway."

Before we knew it, we'd been snatched from the weather, past the inflexible figure of Simmons, into the glow of the kitchen at the rear of the house. Well, we warmed by the fire and ate toast with real jam on it, and swallowed cups and cups of hot tea with honey. Mr. Simmons had disappeared, so we weren't scared to sit there and thaw out a little.

Thawing out ain't the same as enjoying yourself, though. Nope. I for one wasn't about to let down my guard just yet. Cook seemed nice, but I couldn't help wondering what would come next. Ain't nothing had been said about if we was welcome for the night. And Cook was leaving in the morning anyhow. Also, I still hadn't got my head to grasp that we'd truly gone and missed the train. It wasn't the trip or the West I was mourning at all, though. It was missing Miss Blackman. I hadn't realized she'd gotten under my skin so. That cold fact needed some hard private thinking.

Mandy, she was looking down, too. It'd been she that was responsible for talking me back. And here we were, back, only there weren't no future in it. Then again, if I hadn't gone and rescued her, we both could've been on that trip this very minute. I reached for another slice of toast, wondering about Zeb and his mice off and away on that train. It almost made me green, thinking on it. Almost even made me slap down that bread again, uneaten. But then, events being what they was, there was no point in missing a full stomach. No point whatsoever. I ate the last piece of bread, slathered over with more strawberry jam than I'd seen in years. It went down like sawdust.

We didn't see any more of Simmons that evening. Cook put us to bed, Mandy in a cot next to me in that same long dormitory room. It seemed full of ghosts now. I knew Mandy felt it, too, 'cause soon as Cook had disappeared Mandy crawled in beside me. I jumped out for an extra blanket, then tucked us both up.

"It didn't work out right, did it, Jack?"

"I can't say that it did, Mandy."

"Where do you think they are by now, Jack? Your Miss Blackman, and the boy with the mice. What were their names?"

"Tit an' Tat."

"I did so want to meet them."

I ignored that. I weren't up to thinking on Tit and Tat snuggled in Zeb's pocket whilst that train was clacking down the line, whistling long and low into the night. "Probably in western Pennsylvania, by the look of the map in our book. Maybe even Ohio."

"I guess we'll never see those places now, will we?"

"Maybe it just weren't meant to be, Mandy. Maybe

once we'd got out there nobody'd want to adopt us anyhow."

"They didn't even ask me my name, Jack. Not even Cook. I cut my hair off for nothing."

I could feel the sobs ready to burst out.

" 'Tain't so. For one thing, you'd never be bunking here. You'd be off in another great empty room, snuffling to yourself. Leastways, you still got me."

"You mean we've still got each other, Jack."

I guess the thought comforted her some, because she hushed up, and soon I heard her even sleep sounds. It took me a long time to follow suit, though. I just lay there cogitating on the emptiness of the room that by rights should of been full of softly snoring orphans. I even missed the hacks of the consumptive ones. Warm as we were, it weren't a good night.

Cook snuck us each an egg with our gruel in the morning. She said as how they'd just go to waste in the pantry with her off and gone. She was in her traveling clothes, hat and all, as she fried them. They started out sunny side up, then before I could protest, Cook turned them over and squashed them flat in the pan. The one I got on my plate looked like I felt, kind of mangled and all the shine took out of it.

When we was finished, Simmons summoned us to his lair. Cook picked up her valise, then marched the two of us off to a little room off the vestibule where Simmons was waiting. He was sitting with his back to us, hunched over a bunch of papers in a big rolltop desk.

We all three waited a long minute and he didn't take

55

no notice of us, so Cook finally spoke up. "I'm off to my daughter's in Jersey, Mr. Simmons. These two are yours now."

That woke him up. He spun around. "You can't just leave them with me like that, Cook! My whole staff is gone! Miss Gertrude, Miss Blackman, all the maids . . . And you know I was going off to Berkeley Springs myself to soak my rheumatism."

"Can't leave you, can I? Whyever not? It's not me that's in charge of this here philanthropy. You wanted orphans, you got 'em. I only feed 'em. My daughter's waiting on me to help out with her new babe. I'll be back in three weeks, like we agreed."

"You will wait outside until I have finished, Cook Murphy, or there will be no position for you to return to in three weeks."

Well, that seemed clear enough. Cook picked up her bag with a snort and sashayed out, leaving us alone with him.

I looked Simmons in the eye and for a moment he seemed so helpless I almost felt sorry for him. Maybe rheumatism did that to a body, making it all cranky and unbending like that. It was lucky I didn't waste no time following that thought through, though, 'cause his true colors come out soon enough.

I opened my mouth to try and thank him for the food and bed, like my ma would've expected me to, but he gave me a glance that dried up the thanks in my throat and set to with us. "I am not accustomed to wasting my time in conversation with riffraff, so we will make this brief. You. The bigger one. You seem to be the spokes-man. Refresh me on your names."

I gulped. "Jack McConnell, sir. And this is my cousin Mand—, er, Manny Kerrigan. I couldn't sleep the other night just worrying over him. There wasn't nothing to do but go and fetch him so's we could travel West together. But that didn't seem to pan out—"

He waved his hand to silence me. "McConnell, is it? The name seems to ring a bell." He turned to shuffle at the piles on his desk, then bent down to pick up a parcel wrapped in brown paper from the floor. "Miss Blackman was concerned over your absence without leave. She apparently saw something in you that evades me. At any rate, she left this with me, should you decide to grace us with your presence here again."

I reached for the parcel he shoved at me, anxious to open it, yet afraid in his presence. It was heavy, and had the comforting feel and hardness of books. Could it be? Had Miss Blackman remembered, after all? Mandy darted a questioning look at me and I shrugged a shoulder.

Then Simmons opened up again. "I have no staff, and was planning on shutting the house and vacating the city myself, as you heard. You wouldn't care to make a rec-ommendation as to your disposition?"

His voice was dry, but I'd been around long enough to catch the tone in it. It was a tone I'd heard often enough while polishing the boots of gentlemen swells.

Before he could go on, Mandy unexpectedly rushed in. "You needn't worry about us, Mr. Simmons, sir. Jack and me can just go back on the street. We know how to take care of ourselves. If you'd just give us a blanket to take the place of the one you took from Jack when he first got here, it would fix us up. It would be fair, and we don't want anything else."

"Well." Simmons looked at her harder. "It can talk, after all. Unfortunately, I cannot just hand you a blanket and write you off. My sense of moral proprieties would not allow for that. Particularly with the thermometer about to plummet again. Or so the morning papers claim. I fear I shall have to find a slightly better solution to the problem."

He turned to shuffle distractedly through his paperwork once more, then rose with a new determination. "Possibly the answer is at hand, after all."

He went to the door then and summoned Cook. She came, looking put out.

"Cook, what do you suppose your daughter would accept for boarding these urchins for three weeks until my staff returns?"

Cook grunted, then began to get an interested look on her face. I could almost picture things spinning and clicking in her head, like an abacus I seen used once in Chinatown. A bunch of little green balls shoved to one side, then some red ones above and a black or two below.

She finished her figuring. "Sixteen dollars each."

"That's blackmail, pure and simple, and you know it, Cook Murphy."

"It ain't, and that's so. It's what any respectable boardinghouse would get for a double room with meals per month."

"But these children can be persuaded to do useful chores around the house."

"My daughter's already got enough youngsters for that. These two would be a superfluity, and that's God's truth. And her with a new babe to deal with."

"Ten dollars each, and you're still robbing me blind."

"Fifteen."

Well, that went on for a while, till they finally settled on twelve-fifty. Then Simmons turned back to his desk like it was all finished and done with. But Cook, she don't budge.

Simmons finally turned around again. "What is it now, Cook?"

"It's the cash I'll be needing up front, Mr. Simmons, sir."

She said it so calm, but there was iron beneath her voice, too, so I was already beginning to doubt the felicity of the arrangement for Mandy and me.

He glared at her, then finally opened one of the cubbyholes in that desk with a little key from his watch fob, and pulled out a bigger wad of money than I'd ever seen. He counted her fee out slowly, dollar by dollar, like each bill hurt him to pass over. Cook, she snatched it all up with a victorious look, then dragged us out for our coats. Outside on the sidewalk she made us follow her to the trolley stop, and before you know it, we was on our way to the Jersey City ferry.

Chapter 4

I NEVER HAD BEEN across the Hudson be-
fore, but Jersey City weren't no revelation. It turned
out Cook Murphy's daughter lived in a row of factory
houses. Granted, hers was two stories and brick, but it still
wasn't much over the tenements me and Mandy grew up
in. And children! Simmons could of stocked a whole train-
car full from the lot in that house. Cook's daughter hardly looked at us twice, but she grabbed the money fast
enough. Leastways, the twenty dollars that was offered up.
We never did find out what Cook did with the other five.

It was suppertime till things was sorted out, and we
crowded in around a long board table. Cabbage and potatoes. Then Mandy and I were given blankets and told
to bunk down in the pantry.

"And keep your hands off the vittles!"

My quick survey of the shelves with their meager jars
of food and the bins of roots and such below must of tipped
off Cook.

It was cold, away from any of the stoves, but we welcomed
the privacy. It seemed like the first we'd had in a while.

When the rest of the family had bundled off upstairs, I snuck a lantern from the kitchen and we finally got to open up Miss Blackman's package. It was my books, after all. The Dickens and the dream book, and something else, too. The something else was a slim volume bound up in a kind of soft, velvety green flannel. It was stamped on the front in gold: *Excerpts from the Poems of John Greenleaf Whittier.*

I looked inside right off, and there was a signature, soft, but not too flowery, that could only belong to my Miss Blackman: "Property of Angeline Blackman." I sighed and passed it over for Mandy to see. It was a perfect name for her, just like I'd known it would be. Then I reached into a bin for a forbidden apple and crunched into its tartness with satisfaction.

Mandy gave the book a jiggle as she caught it, and a piece of paper fell out. We held it up to the light together. "Dear Jack," it said, "I don't know what happened to make you disappear, but I had a feeling about you, and it won't leave me. In case you do return, I wanted you to have this little book, to keep with your others." Then she signed her name again, "Your friend, Angeline Blackman." And underneath there was one more thing. It must of been a quote from the poems:

> . . . of all sad words of tongue or pen,
> The saddest are these: "It might have been!"

I didn't feel like cogitating on the meaning of that right then and there. The past few days had been bad enough. So Mandy and I bunched together and read *Snow-Bound* until we couldn't keep our eyes open anymore.

Living at the Morresseys' house—for that was their
name—wasn't so bad the first few days. The grub wasn't
prime, and there wasn't a lot of it, what with all the mouths
to feed, but we learned how to grab as fast as the other
ten youngsters. The new baby wasn't up to grabbing yet,
so didn't give us any competition.

We hardly saw much of Mrs. Morressey, for she was
tucked up in her room, getting over her latest birthing.
Cook kept the household going, and kept us busy fetching
coal and helping in the kitchen. She wasn't ever really
mean, and didn't seem to play favorites. She was more
like a stern general keeping her army in line. Of Mr.
Morressey, the father of this brood, we heard not a word,
till he stumbled into the house the third night during
supper, blind drunk.

He was a big, ugly man; hairy, with arms like hams,
and a face already lined with red veins from his drinking.
And he was confused, too. He stood there a moment
counting heads, looking all the time more and more confused.

Suddenly he bawled out: "Where did the extras come
from? I swear on my manhood I only ever begot eleven!
And that eleven too many!"

All his youngsters, from little on up, had hushed up
real fast the moment they heard him barrel in the door.
Now you could see them bunching close to each other
on the benches, cowering in fright. He weren't the sort
of man you'd want to bump into in a dark alley at
night.

But Cook, she acted like nothing unusual was going

on. She just puffed her bosom out a little more prominent and spoke up. "You ain't no more drunk than usual, Liam Morressey. Not that I'd be surprised if you'd counted double up to twenty-four in your state. The extra two is payin' boarders. And they paid well, too."

"Is that a fact?" Some of the hostility left him now, to be replaced by a certain look of cunning. He staggered to the opposite end of the table from Cook and settled into what must have been his chair when he chose to grace it. "And where might this board money be?"

"You're lookin' at it and feelin' it. You ain't been home with your pay for a week. The rent was due. The vittles were low, and the coal bin was near dry. The found money's all gone, and the midwife for your latest babe not even paid yet."

His fists came down on the table with a thunderous bang that set the crockery to shaking. The voice that followed it was almost mellow, though. "And who have I to thank, Mother Murphy, for your annual visits to my home—and your annual meddling?"

"No one but yourself, Liam Morressey, and your annual gift of babes to my poor wore-out daughter."

That thought shifted through his sodden brain but briefly. "Who are these boarders, then?"

Cook shrugged, as if unsure over what to do with a man who couldn't even recognize his own offspring. Then she pointed to Mandy and me.

"Up!" he bellowed at us.

We scuttled off the bench fast, both of us.

"Off with you. Now! You'll not be taking any more food from my table, nor whiskey from my mouth."

"Liam Morressey, they're full paid up for another two and a half weeks!"

The fists landed on the table again, and I could feel Mandy quaking next to me. I guess she figured they might be landing on us next. She was probably right.

I looked for the best avenue of escape, but Cook tried once more. "Those children will not be thrown out into the cold of night!"

"Another word, just one more, and you'll follow them, Mother Murphy." He shoved his empty plate near clean across the table. "Serve me. And get them out of here before I'm finished."

Mandy and me had had enough, anyway. We ran for the pantry to gather our things. I threw everything of ours into one blanket, then filled the other with anything I could grab from the shelves—apples, carrots, potatoes, even a crock of jam. I checked over my clothes to be sure everything was there, too. Pocketknife, bits of string, the key around my neck.

Cook caught us by the back door. It almost looked like there were tears in her eyes. I guess she wasn't such a bad sort. Push come to shove, she just had to stand up for her daughter and grandchildren first. But thank God I hadn't been born into this family. Being on the streets looked to be up from here.

I swung my filled blanket to my shoulder almost apologetically. "Manny and me, we figure the blankets've been paid for, fair and square. We ain't took nothing that didn't belong to us."

"You poor things. Sure and I never meant for this to happen. You see how bad my daughter needed Mr. Simmons's money, don't you? You see what it's like for her."

Cook rummaged in her apron pocket and pulled out a huge handkerchief to blow her nose. She returned it and groped around the pocket some more, finally fishing out two coins. "Here's all I can spare. Take it, and God bless you both."

I grabbed the coins—they were quarters, from the feel of them—and we turned to leave. We didn't get out into the night a moment too soon, either. As the door slammed behind us, I heard Morressey banging into the kitchen. "They're gone? Then that's two bastards less. The devil only knows I'd like to be rid of the rest as easy."

Not knowing anything better, Mandy and me headed for the Hudson River and the ferryboat. Cook's coins came in handy, for once you'd paid your fare, you could ride back and forth on the boat all night if you'd a mind. We stood up the first time across, letting the cold wind with bits of sleet blow the Morresseys out of our heads. They wasn't all cleared out before we got to New York, though, so we stayed put and started back across to Jersey again.

I was fiddling with the change from our fares, kind of tossing the nickel up and down, considering, when the thought come to me. "That's a mighty snug lifeboat they got there, Mandy."

She looked past the rail at the boat just sitting there on its winches, a tarpaulin pulled tight over its top. "We've got blankets tonight, Jack."

"Yup. And you did remark on how it was a pity that boat in Central Park was all froze up in ice."

She looked around, fast, to make certain no one was

watching us. It hardly mattered. It was a filthy night any way you looked at it, and the late passengers was mostly holed up in the smoking saloon.

"Spring or summer would be nicer, but I'd still love being rocked to sleep by the water. Real waves the river's got, too. Much better than that damp pantry at the Morresseys'. And they had cockroaches."

I grinned. "My sentiments precisely. But before we retire, my dear—" She giggled at my words. It was a phrase I'd heard once in a posh play on the Bowery. It'd cost me near fifty cents to see the thing, but it was worth it for this moment. "Before we retire to our bedchamber, we have a little decision to make."

I flipped the coin again and caught it expertly. I was beginning to enjoy myself again. Who needed grownups or the Children's Aid Society? We were on our own again, and it felt good. A surge of energy came over me with the wind biting across my face. Mandy caught my mood. I nodded out to the river surrounding us. The lights of Manhattan shone on one side, the cliffs of New Jersey on the other. We were exactly midway. A good point.

"Anything keeping us in New York?"

"Jack! You mean we might, by ourselves—"

She gave a little hop of excitement. I turned solemn. "I'm going to flip this coin once more, Mandy, as a sign. With your permission." I made a little bow. "Heads, we go back to New York in the morning. Tails, we get off in Jersey and try our luck anywhere else."

Mandy curtsied. It looked funny in her boy's coat and britches. But I didn't giggle again. No, sir. Something important was about to happen. I could feel it.

Then she couldn't stand it anymore. "Toss the coin, Jack. Please. I swear to follow you and the coin's decision faithfully."

"Until death?"

"Until death."

We both crossed our hearts, with me throwing in a good spit for extra certainty. I flipped the coin. It landed in the palm of my right hand and I slapped it on top of the left. Then we both peered through the dark at the nickel. The Liberty Head was buried, and the big "V" for five stared up at us, large as life.

"That's it, then. Tails. It's on the road for us."

We gave each other a little hug, then Mandy pulled me into a dance. I had to stop her when the boat lurched into its docking place. We scrambled for the lifeboat whilst the other passengers hurried to disembark. They were in a rush to return to their old lives. We were feeling reborn. Least, I was.

Mandy, she was just set on having the last word. "Jack?"

"What now?"

"If we'd of flipped that coin on the Jersey side to begin with, we'd have saved twenty cents."

```
,-,-,-,-,-,-,-,-,-,-,
```
Chapter 5
```
,-,-,-,-,-,-,-,-,-,-,
```

I SHOULD'VE KNOWN that last comment of
Mandy's weren't any slip of the tongue. Now that we'd
really decided to be on our own, she took the practicalities
downright serious. First thing Mandy insisted on come
morning was us getting together a little bankroll before
we moved on. Jersey City turned into the right place for
that. Whilst it wouldn't do us no good to try to sell papers
or black boots there, it did have one thing aplenty:
factories.

I kept Mandy and our belongings outside the first one
we came to, while I sashayed right into the employment
office. It was a silk mill, and the noise coming through
from the workrooms was enough to set you deaf. The office
folks spoke up loud enough for me to hear, though. They
wanted to be sure and certain I was over ten. I assured
them I was well past twelve, just a little underfed. They
hired me then and there, fifty cents for an eleven-hour
day, and said I could start on in and they'd only dock me
a dime for the time lost that day.

So then I excused myself and went out for Mandy.

"Listen up, girl. You have to let on you're ten years old for a job. Think you can do it?"

Mandy, she just sniffed and waltzed in for her interview. She came back pleased as punch, and soon we were stashing our blankets in a corner of a vast room vibrating with all the shuttlecocks going every which way. It was a wonder to look at, from the long leather bands running across the ceiling connecting all the machines, right down to the sweating men and women and children. But I didn't get much time to gape. Before I knew it, I was shoving around a huge bin on wheels—the size of a small freight car, it seemed like—taking supplies from machine to machine, while Mandy got instructions on watching over one of them.

That night, out of work long after the early winter dark, we spread our blankets in a hidden corner of the mill yard, behind some rusting machinery, but just inside the gate so's the mill bell would be sure to wake us up. We could hardly stay awake long enough to chew on the Morresseys' raw carrots and apples.

It went like that till payday.

Mandy didn't say a lot about her job, but it didn't take me long to figure out that even with all my pushing of that cart, I got the easier of the two positions. Making my rounds on the floor, I got by Mandy maybe once every hour or so. I always had to stop to check and see if she was all right. She wasn't the only little one at work, but to watch her small body overshadowed by that gigantic loom in front of her was still worrisome.

The warps of the silk stretched out above her, with the shuttles weaving back and forth like crazy to make the cloth. All she had to do was stop the machine with her hand brake every so often to refill the spools when they got empty, but onct in a while the loom went plumb crazy and just smashed threads all over. Then she had to go behind the loom and start tying all the loose ends together, and push 'em through the warp to the front, trying to hide the hole that would be made in the cloth. I lived in fear that the machine might start up of its own accord sometime whilst she was doing this, and weave parts of her right into the cloth.

It was the second day we were on the job and I had just delivered some new thread filling to the loom aside of Mandy when she finished up her bolt. I'd already learned that meant one of the men who worked in the place had to come by and put a new warp in. I smiled at Mandy while she was enjoying this breather and got set to push off down the aisle again, when the warp man arrived. One look, and I froze in my boots. It weren't nobody but Mr. Morressey himself, stripped down to just boots, britches, and long johns in the heat of the place. I cast a quick glance at Mandy and saw that she'd made the identification same as me. She was looking green around the gills. There weren't no way we could do much communicating in that overall din, so I just sort of slunk around my bin and tried to make myself smaller than I already was. Mandy hadn't any place to hide, though.

Would he recognize us?

It was a tense few minutes watching and waiting while he did the job. But the whole time he acted like Mandy wasn't even there. He did manage to give a pinch to the bottom of a young woman next door to Mandy, though, afore he left. She didn't seem to mind too much, just took it in stride. Then he was gone. But just the fact of his being in that factory ruined the rest of my day.

It also became the main subject of Mandy's and my supper conversation out in the mill yard that night. There we sat, eating Morressey's vittles, scared silly to come out from behind the junk pile in case he could be wandering around.

"You think he might recognize us, Jack?"

"Small chance, if he couldn't even separate us from his own children."

"And he was really drunk the other night."

"Looked hung over today, too."

"Not too hung over to pester poor Mildred next to me. She says he does that to all the women."

"Why do they have to put up with it?"

"Who will they complain to, the foreman? He's as big as Mr. Morressey, and a friend of his, too, Mildred says. She's afraid she'll lose her job."

"I can't stand a man who takes advantage of women and children," I throw in. "Nothing but grownup bullies. There's got to be a better class of manhood out there."

"We haven't met any yet, Jack."

Then she gave me a serious look. "You're not going to grow into one them, Jack, are you? I couldn't stand it."

Well, I just gave the girl an insulted look and pulled the blanket over my head. I thought she had more faith in me than that. She had to apologize three times before we made up.

I started to keep an eye on Morressey around the floor after that. I figured if I knew where he was he couldn't sneak up on me and give me any surprises. We only tangled once, though, when he figured I didn't come to fetch a bolt of silk from a loom fast enough to suit him.

Then he looked at me hard for the first time. "You new here, boy?"

"Yes, sir."

"Ain't I seen you somewheres before?"

"Don't think so, sir." He hadn't been seeing very well that night at his house, after all.

"You only get one warning. Trot right fast when I call. I don't put up with no guff from children."

"Yes, sir. No, sir." And I sped away from his huge arms and beer belly. I figured he couldn't beat me up too hard there in front of everybody, but I wasn't noways willing to give him a chance to try.

Well, the week dragged itself on and out, the two of us living on Morressey leftovers and a few loaves of bread we bought with the last thirty cents from Cook, until it's finally Saturday and payday. We stood in line like everybody else for our little pay envelopes, then took a last look behind us at the now silent workrooms.

"I guess my idea about a bankroll wasn't so great, Jack," Mandy said to me as we stood there, the clatter of the machines still ringing in our ears like ghosts to haunt us. "Or maybe it was just the way we picked. There's got to be a better way to make some money."

I just slowly poured the coins in my envelope onto my hand and counted them. "I never worked so hard for two dollars and ninety cents in my life. And the noise of mills clutters up your mind so you can't even think. No wonder Morressey drinks."

"It ain't no kind of freedom at all, Jack."

I couldn't do naught but agree. Sunday morning we left Jersey City and I hoped to never see it again.

The day was cold, but the sun was shining, and that braced us some. We walked out into the country and just kept going, in the complete opposite direction from the Hudson River, which was bound to be west. It was kind of like Central Park, only more of it, as far as you could see, except there were milk cows instead of sheep. And that became a lucky thing.

Since it was Sunday, and the few village stores we passed were closed, there was no place to spend any of our money on vittles, and by nightfall our morning excitement was long gone. We were near ready to drop from hunger and thirst. There was still one potato left from the Morresseys', true, but we neither of us had the appetite for another raw potato. We were still a little leery of grownups, too, figuring maybe we were a mite too close yet to New York for them to be much different from the city variety we been experiencing. So we kept our distance from them, and kept walking till I spotted a working barn that was built a fair distance from its owner's house.

"How about we hole up in there for the night? There must be some straw or something to sleep in, and we'd have a roof over our heads."

"I could sleep right here on my feet, Jack, if only my stomach weren't paining me so."

I didn't even try to come up with an answer for that. My stomach felt the same. We skirted around the far side of the house and snuck into the barn. It being the first barn I ever been privy to, I kind of stopped and felt it out. It weren't much warmer than outside, that was sure. There were maybe one-inch gaps between every blessed board on its walls. The full moon that just come out from behind some clouds was blasting in through those gaps, along with a stiff little wind that started kicking up the last half hour.

There was another thing, which Mandy noticed, too. "It stinks in here, Jack!"

"Won't help to wrinkle up your nose like that, Mandy. I guess farmers don't have time to bathe their livestock onct a week like you insist on us doing. We'll probably get used to it. They must."

She pouted. "Since you think you know so much about farmers all of a sudden, maybe you can tell if there's anything good to eat around here!"

"Simmer down. I'm hungry, too." I went poking my head into the first open stall and almost got kicked by the hind end of a huge old horse for my efforts. I quickly moved on down the line. The rest was all cows, sort of half sleeping and making soft animal sounds.

"Cows, is all."

"I can see that!" Then she looked closer at one and pointed. "Look there, Jack, at those things hanging down from it."

I looked. "What of them?"

74

"Do you suppose—" She stopped in embarrassment. "Well, milk has to come from somewhere, doesn't it?"

I took another gander at the cow in question, down at the things, then back to the rest of the cow again, all thousand pounds or so of it. "That may be so, then again it mayn't. Either way, I ain't nohow getting myself killed finding out. I'm not *that* hungry!"

Mandy glanced at me like maybe I'm not her favorite hero anymore, but I wouldn't be moved. Enough is enough. So we trotted through the rest of the barn until we found a little door near the back. I gave it a try and it opened. The moonbeams shining through the slats of the wall were reflecting all over a dozen or so big silvery canisters.

"Will you look at that!"

"Milk cans, Jack, like the ones they carted down Delancey Street every morning!"

I didn't even stop to think about could they be empty. I just hauled off the lid of the nearest one. It was good and full, with all the cream thickened up right around the top. Suddenly we were both laughing. The sight of food did that to us a lot lately.

I held her back before she drownded herself in it. "See anything against your morals here, Mandy?"

"Don't be silly, Jack. After we get our fill, there'll still be enough milk and cream here for the entire city of New York!"

Come Monday morning, we hit a fresh town.

Mandy looked at the town, then at me, like she'd made a decision. "Jack, I'm tired of carrying this blanket so.

75

I'm taking my money and spending it to make things easier."

Well, that made a certain amount of sense. The truck in my blanket had been feeling more like lead every minute, but I weren't about to admit it, not having come upon a solution myself. So I shrugged and threw in my pay, too. "I just hope you save some of that for vittles, girl."

"We can always find something like we did last night, Jack. If we spend our pay on food now, like we could easy, where will we be? Back where we started, that's where. And we'd only get hungry again in a few days."

She was probably right, but it still hurt to watch what she did with all my wages from that terrible week at the silk mill. She stopped in a general merchandise store and spent near all of it on scissors and needles and thread and such, and a pot, too. She would of forgotten the matches we were in dire need of if I hadn't made a point of bringing them up. At least she saved enough for us to go into a little eatery and fill up on hot soup, it being a long time gone since our breakfast of cow's milk.

"What we need, Jack—" She was still acting in charge, between spoonfuls of the thick bean soup. "What we need is something easy to carry our things in for journeying. And I need a place to cut it out and sew it together. A place where my fingers won't freeze up while I'm doing it."

"You got in mind a kind of knapsack?"

She smiled and swallowed. "One for you and one for me. I think I can manage two out of one blanket."

"It'll be colder nights."

"It's March already. Spring's got to be coming on."

It seemed to me I used that line of reasoning last time, and she didn't accept it then. But anyways I let her have the point and we scraped our bowls clean and moved out.

What we found was another barn, an abandoned one a couple miles out of town. It'd long since lost its coat of white paint, and was leaning treacherously every which way, but it was shelter of a sort. I did kind of miss the gentle animal snuffles that had put us to sleep in that other barn's loft last night, though. But Mandy was already fired up with her project and didn't seem to notice. I watched her lay out the best blanket—the one without the holes—and set to figuring on it like she'd be all day. I shrugged and set up a fire close to her work, to give her a little more light, and maybe keep her warm, as well. There was lots of old hay around for tinder, and fallen-down boards, too.

Looking at that fire shaping up made me think of food, as usual. That soup had gone down too fast. "You suppose there's anything to eat around here, Mandy?"

She didn't even look up from her thinking, just smiled and answered sweetly, "You're the man of the family, Jack. See what you can find."

So I did. I went out and found a little gurgling crick and filled up the new pot with water from it, then set it on the fire to boil up with our last potato. Everything else was gone. Then I had to think hard. What did they have eatable in the country toward the end of winter?

Outside, the sun was shining kind of pale and weak, and that March wind was still up, but at least it weren't raining or snowing. The fields around went into little hills.

They looked like they hadn't been farmed for a while. Rabbits, maybe? I'd heard tell of rabbits but hadn't ever faced up with one. Neither did I have any idea how to catch one if I did. I was born and bred city, after all. It was almost naked I was beginning to feel, without the shelter and protection of all those New York buildings around me. I stood in the middle of an empty field in that thin light just considering it all. Then it got to be too much to think on all by myself and I gave up on sighting a rabbit and went into the barn to have it out with Mandy.

She was still concentrating hard, measuring and marking with a bit of pencil stub from our stash, and a cloth measuring tape she'd picked out at the store.

"Mandy, we've got to talk."

"Ssh. I've just got it where I can start in cutting."

"Mandy, stop acting like a silly female and give me your time. That'll keep another little while."

She put down the pencil with a slight frown. It made her look so grown up, that frown did, that I almost bust out laughing.

"All right, Jack. Though I was trying to ease our life some."

"That's what we need to talk on. Our life." I poked into the pot that was starting to boil up now. It looked like a half a potato each and some vegetable broth was what we'd be getting. A cooked potato had to be better than raw, though, like we'd gotten fed up on eating in the mill yard. Even without salt.

Mandy gave an impatient little sigh and I directed my attention back to her. "It ain't simple, you know, girl. Being the head of this team and all. And the last day and a half I get the feeling that we ain't exactly been directing ourselves with a purpose. I mean, we just been walking, farther and farther away from anything we know about."

"But you flipped the coin! I only agreed to abide by it."

"I know, I know." I was walking around her little rectangle of marked-up blanket now. It ain't always easy, coming up with the right words to think things out, either. "Dash it, Mandy, we got to have a plan!"

"Like what, Jack?"

Here I was, getting all het up, and she just sat there on the hard-packed dirt of the barn floor, giving me that innocent, trusting look. I raked my fingers through my hair in frustration, then my fingers touched on the string still hanging round my neck. I fumbled it all the way out.

"What's this key mean to you, girl?"

"Why, it means a place we were happy together."

"Don't it mean anything else?"

She thought; then, "I guess it means we have to search for the place where it fits in again. To open another door." She looked down at the old gray blanket. "A place we won't have to leave again."

"Tell me what we're searching for, Mandy!"

"We're searching for a ho—" She stumbled over the word like it was hard to say. "A home, Jack. And maybe —maybe someone nice to look after us for a while . . ." There were tears sprouting now. "Oh, Jack, I'm ever so tired of us looking after ourselves all the time! I know we're nothing special, I mean there are so many like us living on the streets in New York, and we don't deserve parents any more than they do, but it would be so nice! And I know it's hard to come by good grownups, so it's not the best I'd be willing to settle for . . . Just someone who'd keep us warm and feed us once in a while, and didn't beat us . . ." As that seemed an impossibility in itself, she just stopped there.

"What if," I continued relentlessly, "what if we don't ever find someone like that? Or someone better than that? Someone like Miss Blackman, say?"

Her eyes lit up at the mention of Miss Blackman. I'd described her so many times that to Mandy she was like that angel on the ceiling in our old house. An impossible, protective, beatific presence.

"Then we'll just have to do it ourselves, Jack."

And she wiped her eyes on her coat sleeve and bent back over her work.

I walked back outside, unsatisfied. "Home" was too mystical a word for me. I'd called my cubbyhole in the bakery home, and our town house in New York. I was afraid to use or even think on the word again until I had much more proof that such a thing could exist for real.

I wandered around in the wind until I scraped upon the burnt-out ruins of what must have been the farmhouse on this spread. That was why they'd left.

But was a home just a place? Was it something gone when it burnt down? Or was it more? I walked along the outlines, tracing over the dried weeds that had grown up around the charred board stubs. Then I walked beyond, past where the back door would've been. There was a broken-down well, and another patch of dried weeds. I shuffled through them wearily, then bent to look closer.

This must've been the family's kitchen garden, and it'd gone to seed. I rooted around with more will now, and in a few minutes I was racing back to the barn, my arms laden with frostbitten carrots and turnips for the pot.

We ate boiled vegetables twice that day, until we couldn't hold any more. Mandy had one of the knapsacks stitched together and she measured it on me for strap sizes after supper. It felt pretty good, and left my arms free for swinging. I noticed her rubbing her eyes, though.

"Save the other for tomorrow, Mandy. You'll be needing spectacles we can't afford, you keep that up." Then I added, "You did a real nice job."

"You really think so, Jack? I had to triple-stitch all the seams, for strength, and wool isn't easy to work with."

"Where'd you learn to sew so good, anyhow?"

"My pa used to lend me out to a lady next door in our tenement. She took in piecework from the sweats. She paid pa half what she got for the stuff I did—men's trousers, mostly. She said the other half went toward the time it took up, her teaching me how."

"Well, I guess she taught you all right, anyway."

Mandy rubbed her eyes some more. "All afternoon I've been thinking about what you were trying to say, Jack. About what we've got to do. Sewing frees up your head for that."

"And?"

"And, well, maybe we ought to put some kind of end to what we're looking for. I mean, we could just keep on walking forever, couldn't we? And we still wouldn't be out West."

"Out West. Always comes back to that, don't it?" I grumbled.

"How far out West was the train going, Jack? They never talked about it to the girls at the dormitory."

I went for our pile and dug out the dream book. It flipped right open to the big map of the country.

"Look here," I pointed. "Miss Blackman was talking about a place called Nebraska."

We bent over the book, searching for the mysterious name. Mandy found it first. "Here."

Her finger was square on it. I noticed the finger had been bleeding a little around the nail. She must of poked it with the needle. We'd have to maybe see about getting her a thimble next time we was in the money.

"How far you figure that is, Jack? There must be lots of people wanting children in Nebraska if they keep taking trainloads out."

"Too far. A couple thousand miles, easy."

"How far is a mile, Jack?"

"We maybe walked two or three this morning."

"Oh. We'd be grown up and not needing parents anymore when we made it that far."

"You're right there." I settled back on my haunches, ready to give up on the whole thing. But not Mandy. Once she settled her mind to something, she kept right at it with a will. She took to paging through the book, then finally settled on another map. I looked closer. It was a picture of New Jersey and Pennsylvania.

"So?" I said.

"I want a place that's possible, Jack. If you're not

interested, I'm going to pick a place that sounds nice. A place we can walk to from here."

I just watched her studying that map, maybe a little curious about what she'd come up with, but not letting on.

"This is the place!"

"Where?"

I inched closer to see where her finger was now. She moved it away so I could read the tiny print.

"New Hope. New Hope, Pennsylvania. Doesn't it have a nice sound to it, Jack?"

"It does at that. But it's also, let's see, about a fifty-mile walk, and on the other side of a big river." My nose was practically on top of the map now. It was time to tend the fire again. The night blackness around us in the barn was getting deeper. "The Delaware." I looked up. "You couldn't have picked something closer, could you?"

"Nope. New Hope sounds just perfect."

"All right, then. We pull out as soon as you've got the traveling gear finished."

Chapter 6

WE LOADED OURSELVES down with as many root vegetables as we could carry the next day, and started out just before noon, as soon as Mandy had finished the second knapsack. It was another cold day, this time more overcast, but the walking seemed easier with our new packs. We stopped in a town we came to for some soup bones and a twist of salt, and that's as far as our factory money went. By rationing out the bones, we figured we'd have enough for a pot of soup each day. Sleeping nights mostly in haystacks, on account of grown-ups still made us wary, and there weren't any safe-looking barns, we made it to the Delaware River in about five days. Five days of nothing but marching with one foot in front of the other.

Somehow, the Delaware River had set itself up in our minds as a dividing line for our travels, and our feelings. Somehow, we figured that once we made it to the other side of that river it would be safe to stop ducking into hedges when questionable-looking wagons and carriages come down the road. I'm not sure why, but the other side of the Delaware, and New Hope sitting by it, was where we intended to give the human race a second chance.

Naturally, with all that at the back of our minds, just crossing that river took on a special kind of meaning for both of us. There wasn't nothing going to get in our way of making that crossing. Somewhere on the other side of the river was New Hope. How to get across was the problem.

We found a ferry, but its master wasn't having any truck with free rides for orphan children. The fact is, after his first refusal we'd gone around his back and tried to stow away behind some boxes on the craft. He was a sharp 'un, though, and spotted us just before clearing the shore. He pulled me out by the hair and gave me a kick with his boot that made it hard to consider sitting for a few hours. Afterwards, Mandy figured that ferrymaster for living on the New Jersey side of the Delaware. I sincerely hoped so, but was beginning to suspicion that one single river wasn't going to change the behavior of grownups as much as we'd have liked.

We walked some more, south along the river, following the currents, and found a bridge at Frenchtown, only it was a toll bridge, so that was out, too. But at least Frenchtown was on the map in our book, so we could see that New Hope wasn't more than maybe eight miles from us— across the river and down it.

Feeling discouraged so near to our goal, we walked another four or five miles, staying always as close to the water as the forest around would let us, and finally come to a couple of rowboats pulled up out of the water, on a sandy bank under winter-bare trees. They was a little

85

rickety, and filled with about a foot of dirty snow and new rain, but looked to be seaworthy.

I was just standing there like a pillar of stone, cogitating on them boats, when Mandy spoke up. "If they still belonged to somebody, they wouldn't be sitting here all winter long gathering leaves and snow, would they, Jack?"

"You got a point, Mandy. If they was my boats, I would've hauled 'em up off the bank way before winter, in case of flooding and all. I'd of tipped 'em over, or at least covered 'em up with canvas like the ones in Central Park. So they wouldn't look abandoned. A sad thing it is, to see boats look so let down and derelict like these."

By now Mandy was poking at the front of the better-looking of the two craft, knocking on the wood to see if it was all rotted out or not. It didn't seem to be.

"I truly believe they don't belong to anyone, Jack. And, anyway, we could always bring it back across the river, once we had enough return money for the ferry or one of the toll bridges along here."

"We'd only be borrowing it, is what you're getting at."

She smiled at the word once it was out in the open like that. "We've just *got* to get across that river, Jack. And this boat looks like it's been waiting right here, just for us to borrow it."

The ethics of the enterprise settled to our satisfaction, we hid out till dark, laying for a couple of hours in our blanket in the woods under some bushes, watching that river. As dark came closer, though, and the more I looked at the water, the less I liked the idea.

"You been noticing the way that river runs, Mandy?"

"So fast and free, Jack. It's beautiful!"

"Fast and free ain't the least of it. It's full up with melted snows and the rains from the last few weeks. I even seen a few hunks of ice still coming through from upriver. The currents look mean. And I wouldn't want to play hide-and-seek with any of that there flotsam and jetsam floating past."

"You think we can't do it?"

"I think I've never touched an oar in my life, nor been in a boat that size except to sleep in. I'm thinking we could drown just as easy as getting across."

"But, Jack, it's not *that* far across!"

So then I looked at the Delaware again, figuring on how far it really was to the other side. "Don't look like much by foot, girl, but it ain't on our feet we'll be going. I'll bet it's near a quarter mile to the Pennsylvania side."

She didn't say anything, but her eyes went a little bigger. Must've had something to do with that big tree root that just swept past in front of us.

"All that stuff floating in the water, Jack. Could it hurt us?"

"At the speed it's coming, it'd probably cleave a hole right through one of them paltry rowboats."

"Oh." She thought a while, then: "There was a little cotton mill back there in Frenchtown. Maybe we could go back and get work for a day or two, then cross the toll bridge, then—"

"Forget it. I'm never laying a foot inside another mill. And you neither, if I have anything to do with it. It's a wonder you still got all ten fingers after a week on that loom you had."

"Mildred only had eight. She lost the little one on her right hand to the loom when she was eleven, like you, and one on her left just two years back—"

I gave Mandy a black look. "Enough said. It's New Hope you've set your hat on, and it's there we'll go this very night, river or no."

We dozed off a little, and when we woke, the night had come. I lifted the blanket from my head. Maybe we'd slept harder than I thought. I couldn't get a fix on the time in the gloomy blackness. It was raining again, not just damp like earlier. The blanket was wet clear through. And it wasn't the soft sound of the rain, but that of the river which caught my ear. The same river we'd been watching earlier. How could it sound even more treacherous now?

I nudged Mandy awake. "Time to do it."

She yawned. "Couldn't we have some supper first? My pa always used to say that a condemned man was always given a big meal first. Before they hung him. Or shot him. Or otherwise done him in."

"How would he know?"

"I think maybe he was mixed up in some of those Irish troubles before he ran off to America with my mother. I never did figure out what all he was talking about."

"But I know what you're talking about," I cut in. "Trying to get around setting foot on one of them boats."

She gave me a look. "I really am hungry, Jack! And I really do want to get across that river!"

"All right, I know you're not a shirker. But since there's naught to eat, it don't matter anyhow. Sling on your knapsack and let's go bail."

When the boat was as empty as it was going to get, I set our cooking pot in the front part, in case more bailing would be called for, then gave Mandy a boost into it. I double-checked to be sure and certain the oars was tight in their locks, then pushed as hard as ever I could until I felt the boat start to slip and slide into the water.

"Hurry up, Jack! It's going to take off without you!"

"I'm coming!"

And with a great leap, I was. There was kind of a bump and lurch as we left the land, and I grabbed for the oars as the first current we hit set us to spinning.

"We're going backwards!"

"Hush up. I'll get the hang of these things in a minute."

And I did, sort of. The oars felt a lot bigger and heavier in my hands than I'd expected. And I had to stretch my arms way out to hold on to both of them. I don't think the boat had been designed with an underfed eleven-year-old like me in mind. When I finally got its nose pointed in the right direction, south, I heaved a sigh of relief and started working us toward the center of the river.

The relief was short-lived. The water had taken on new contours, with us sitting in the middle of it like we were. There must've been more than just hard currents running underneath of us. There was waves, real waves, coming up at us, and what I took to be rocks, or maybe ice, to one side. I maneuvered best I could between those impediments and kept straining till my arms felt like they were about to bust out of their sockets. It was all going on for entirely too long. Ten minutes? Fifteen? More like forever.

Then Mandy, sitting in the front watching me, she yelled out. "Behind us! There's something horrible heading right for the boat!"

I twisted my head around, fast. Sure enough, there was something coming for us. A giant tree root? A piece of a house? I couldn't make it out in the black of night, so just rowed like I was possessed, trying to get out of its way. Almost made it, too.

It clipped us from the left, giving us a heaving push toward the Pennsylvania side of the river, then continued on its way. I was about to say thank you, politely, for the good shove, when I noticed the water coming into the boat. It weren't coming from the waves. It was coming from the new hole in the side right between Mandy and me.

"Water, Mandy. Water! Grab the pot!"

Well, she started bailing like crazy, and I'm rowing like my life depended on it, which it no doubt did. Only, the water was coming in faster than Mandy could pitch it out, and I was having a harder time making any progress on account of the boat seemed to be sinking into the river, fast, and my arm muscles hadn't got much more going for them. I gave another great heave on the oars, then felt my right one lodge up against something. That something must of had fingers on it, 'cause it snatched that oar right out of my hand. Now I was rowing like crazy with one oar, not making much headway against the currents, and the top of the boat was slowly but surely sinking down to the water level. Then the entire river came swirling in.

"Mandy! Can you swim?"

"I never tried!"

So I dumped the oar and reached out and grabbed hold of her, hard. We didn't even have to jump out of that boat. It just sort of left us. Then we were in the river. It was even colder than I thought. Ice-cold. Mandy was flailing out, trying her best to do what she considered swimming, but that ain't nowhere near enough to the real thing. I'd got aholt of her by one of her knapsack straps and was barely managing to keep both our heads out of the river. She was heavy, wet like that. I was about ready to bag the whole thing and give up on New Hope and a new future for the two of us when along came a big old log that near busted me in the head. It took me a full minute to latch on to its possibilities and it, but then me and Mandy was both attached, getting a free ride downstream. When that log headed in toward shore and I could feel a sandy bottom beneath my feet again, I was almost froze, but game.

I tugged at Mandy to see if she was still with me. She looked like a half-drownded rat, but she unsquinched her eyes and gave a little smile. "It must be the angel from our old ceiling still looking after us, Jack," she panted out.

"Must be, 'cause I can't think of anybody else that wouldn't have been just as happy to be rid of an extra two orphans."

So we pulled ourselves onto the west bank of the river, then scrambled up the small bluff above it. The wool of our packs was twice as heavy with the extra water it'd sopped up. We tried wringing them out some, and our coats, too, but it didn't do much good. It had started to pour in earnest now anyway. I looked down the muddy dirt road next to the bluff. Buildings of a town were beginning to take shape, just dark shadows through the night and weather.

"Those currents must of brought us further and faster than we expected. Welcome to New Hope, Pennsylvania."

But Mandy didn't pay any mind to my sarcasm. Even through the rain I could see the satisfied look on her face, like she figured we were within touching distance of the Holy Grail or something.

"You really got a feeling about this place, don't you?"

"It's what we fixed on, Jack, and we got here, didn't we? All the way across that raging river. If it was this hard to get to, there's got to be something good waiting for us. We just have to find it."

"But not yet." I hated to squelch her enthusiasms like that, but it was still a good hour or two before daybreak. And that might be hard to see when it came, with the rain and all. "We'll have to wait till people start waking up, then case the place, casual-like."

She sneezed and started hopping up and down, trying to warm up. "Do we have to stand out here in the rain all that time?"

"Gesundheit. Maybe not. Maybe there's a shack or stable or something to shelter us a little." What I was thinking was there'd better be, or the two of us would be near dead of the cold and wet in another little while.

We took one last look at the river before we started sloshing into town.

"It's lucky that there was an abandoned boat. It ain't never getting back to where it came from now."

Mandy had a funny cast to her face and didn't bother making further comment on our borrowed boat.

I poked my nose closer to hers. "With a little light you might look a fine shade of purple. But I'm not sure it would become you." She was shivering, too, so hard it shook her whole body. I was beginning to get worried. My legs felt like they'd got St. Vitus' dance, too. There was nothing for it but to carry on. We did. Straight for the houses that loomed up ahead.

My feet squished around the water and mud in my boots with each step. Being on the road sure had its poor side. I couldn't ever remember being this wet in New York. There was always an awning or tenement hall to slip under or into there. And I hadn't ever figured on rain being more devious than snow. It didn't make sense, but it felt colder for sure. Course, there was the unanticipated swim in the river to be considered. I sneezed.

"God bless you."

"Thanks a bunch."

Misery was settling into every inch of me. I was toying with the idea of just succumbing to a tremendous case of pneumonia or consumption, when we squelched into what must have been the center of town. I sized up the main street the best I could in the gloom. The sky seemed to be lightening. We must've spent more time on the Delaware than I'd estimated. It was probably closer to six in the morning than five.

The buildings was mostly whitewashed and bright, with a few built of stone. They came in clearer every minute as we stood there shivering in the middle of the street.

Old-looking buildings, solid and handsome, with a little space between them. Mandy hadn't picked any factory town, I'd hand her that much. I decided not to kick the bucket just yet and swallowed a fresh sneeze.

"Here, Mandy," I hissed.

"Yes?"

"We ain't never had any luck with the fronts of buildings. Let's trail around back. Might be some warm stables."

We wandered down a side street and into what probably passed as an alley out here. I judged it to be right behind the main street itself. Sure enough, in the struggling light there stood a henhouse and other outbuildings. They weren't shacks, though, none of them. All solid and whitewashed. We'd wandered in off the dirt road onto somebody's private property. It was a big house they all belonged to, with additions jutting out the back on two sides. And in one of the wings we spotted a moving light behind a window.

I pulled Mandy against me. "Hush now. Somebody's waking up." We scuttled into the nearest door, which happened to belong to the outhouse. It was a big one—four holes—and even had a little pile of soft paper sitting at hand. I scarfed a handful to blow my nose, while Mandy tried, with shaking fingers, to wipe down her face.

"You think this is the best place to hide, Jack?"

"What do you mean?" I threw the wad down the nearest gaping hole.

"Wouldn't this be the first place likely for a body to visit on rising?"

"Oh, lordy." I gave myself a whack on the head. "Why didn't I think of that?"

"There are plenty of other sheds outside, Jack. Not that I mind this one. It's the cleanest privy I ever been in, not counting the water closet in our old house."

"All right, all right, we'll move." I creaked open the door to peek out again. A little daylight had started filtering through a high window in the outhouse, but I was still surprised by how bright the sky was getting. Maybe the rain would stop.

"It's getting too light. We'll have to run fast before whoever's up in the big house spots us."

I motioned for Mandy to go out first, and she did, then she stopped cold before me. "Jack. Look! The house!"

I looked. There was smoke swirling around the window where we'd seen the lantern. Thick black smoke. And a flicker of light just beyond it that looked suspiciously like a wild flame.

"Come on!"

I didn't stop to think, just shoved past Mandy and raced up the hill to the back of the house. I looked quickly for a door, but couldn't seem to find one, so I shrugged off my sodden pack and shoved it, hard, through that window. My estimation weren't wrong. The smoke come billowing out, solid and mean. I gave it a second to clear out a bit, then barreled in.

I could just make out the inside of the room now, around the edges of the swirling smoke. I could feel the heat, too. It was a kitchen, and there was somebody cowering off behind the stove by the wall. Something must've stopped up the big flue, and sent sparks flying. They'd caught the curtains already, which was why things was beginning to brighten up now that the smoke had an outlet. Water was what was needed, but not knowing the lay of the land, I used what was still handy, swatting my sodden knapsack up against the flames. That got too heavy, so I stopped to pull off my equally sodden coat and used that.

I hardly noticed, but Mandy had followed me in, and she was doing likewise with a spark that had caught on the oil tablecloth. Well, we ran around like chickens with our heads cut off for a few minutes, then finally noticed the flames was dead, but the smoke still coming. I spied a door to the outside, and flung it open. Coming back, I stumbled over the stove shovel, snatched it up to pry open the stove's firebox, and started in tossing the hot coals out the back door into the rain. When the box was empty, the smoke let up.

By this time I'd sunk down onto the floor, coughing hard. When the hacks eased up, the figure cowering by the far corner wasn't cowering no more. It had stood up and turned into a little old lady, soot from head to toe. Mandy sunk down beside me and the three of us stared at each other for a while.

"Lands. You ain't more than children, the both of you."

Mandy and me, we both jumped a little when her words come out like that.

"And here I thought all the time the Lord had sent me some angels to fight that devil fire, the way you was flying around." She took off her spectacles and gave them a polish with the underside of her apron. Then she set them on her nose again and gave us another look. "Maybe you are cherubs, the little variety. But I never seen pictures of any so skinny, wet, and dirty."

So we set and stared at each other another little while, still catching our breaths.

"Can you talk?"

"Oh, yes, ma'am," said Mandy finally. "And you were just lucky Jack and I were happening by. Jack, he knows fires and ovens better than anybody."

"Is that so, now." She gave me a hard look, then Mandy. "And what would you be doing wandering by in this filthy weather before dawn?"

"This is New Hope, ain't it, ma'am?" Mandy went on. "We come here specifically to find some of it. Jack and me. All the way from New York City."

Well, I struggled up then, muttering about checking out her flue. Before she could stop me, I was outside the door, poking into where it's supposed to let the smoke out. I had a feeling what I was looking for, and before you knew it, my fingers had lodged deep inside the tin pipe, right up to my armpit, and touched on something. I latched on to it and tugged. It pulled out with a plop and I drug it back inside.

"Here's your villain, ma'am. Biggest blackbird I ever seen."

"You really must be from the city. Ain't you ever seen a crow before?"

"No, ma'am, but I reckon I'll recognize it next time. Leastways, if it's as dead as this one."

I threw the poor creature out the door, then the old lady pulled herself together. "Well, sitting around gabbing won't get breakfast on the table for my boarders. And me fixing to do the week's baking today, too."

We followed her eyes over to the dry sink that had a board atop it, covered with lumps of rising dough.

"Do you suppose it can still be salvaged enough to bake?" she wondered aloud.

"I can get your stove going again, ma'am," I piped up. "In no time. The flue should work just fine without that crow stuck up it."

"Well, get on with it then, boy. Jack, is it? And you"— she turned to Mandy—"what's a pretty little thing like you doing in britches? And what have you gone and done to your hair? That's the most pitiful massacree I ever seen. Even the Injuns out West do a finer job on their scalping. I should know. Seen one or two examples back in my salad days with Mr. Bergman, may he rest in peace."

Then we were all scuttling about, fixing up the damage. There weren't nothing more said about Mandy and me, as to our disposition. Weren't even time to figure on how she'd seen clean through Mandy's disguise so fast, when no one else had managed all this time. We were all too busy getting clean and dry and the food done up for Mrs. Bergman's boarders.

"My, but didn't you children eat a nice breakfast. I just love good eaters. Want another dollop of potatoes, my dears?"

"No, thank you, ma'am," I said. We'd got the kitchen back in order, helped with the cooking, and now Mrs.

98

Bergman was feeding us, right at the same table with her four steady boarders. There'd been introductions, but the hot food in front of us wafted the names right out of reach. There was a schoolmaster, a tall, thin, middle-aged man with a prominent nose and a distant look in his eyes. There was also two maiden ladies, and an ancient old geezer who didn't say nothing but made a lot of noise gumming down his food. And such food! There was pancakes, eggs and potatoes, sausages and bacon, the fresh bread hardly worse for its adventure, and lots of trimmings. Not to mention a pitcher full of fresh, creamy milk. I didn't know when I'd be able to stand again, I was that stomach-heavy.

"Well, then, what is it I can get the two of you? It's not every day my home and worthless old self are saved from the conflagration."

"If you're referring to that little fire, ma'am, don't mention it again. It was our sheer pleasure." Then I got an idea and added, bold as brass, "But since you're asking, it's a place to stay we'll be wanting. Wouldn't happen to have a spare bed around here, would you? Mandy and me, we're used to bunking together and aren't hardly no trouble at all, at all. Also we're stronger than we look. We could help with your boarders."

I looked right into Mrs. Bergman's eyes the whole time I was saying this. I could see she was older even than she let on, and maybe getting a little tired from all the work.

And Mandy, she caught on pretty fast to my ploy, too. "I can help with the cooking, and tidying up, and Jack could keep your fires going. He's got more 'sperience with fires than anybody I know. He used to keep a huge bakery oven in New York going all by himself."

"Well, and I guess I can believe that's a true fact."

Mrs. Bergman pulled on some strands of gray hair that were creeping down from her bun, not having had time to spruce herself up more than changing her dress after our adventure. We were all still pretty grubby, for a fact, even though Mandy and me had taken the time to scrub most of the smoke from our hands and faces. But Mrs. Bergman, she must get up hours before her boarders every day to fix all these vittles on her own.

"It has been hard these last few years since Mr. Bergman passed on to his reward and I came back East from Kansas to run this boardinghouse. Of course, I've got two town girls to help me out in the kitchen every so often, but seems to me they spend more time eyeing the occasional young man what comes through. Specially them traveling drummers. It's surprising how many salesmen we get out here, coming through on their way to Philadelphia. It's almost as bad as when we lived just off the main line of the Atchison, Topeka and the Santa Fe." Then she got distracted by an empty platter in front of us and wandered off with it back to the kitchen.

Mandy and me just looked at each other.

"That does it," said I. "Can't stand it no more." And I grabbed Mandy and hauled her off to the kitchen.

Over by the big black stove, Mrs. Bergman was fussing with the coffeepot. She finally noticed us. Mrs. Bergman looked first at Mandy, still in her boy's britches, then at me. "I want you to know I'm a grandmother. Five times already. I'm much too old for mothering." Then she sighed. "Come here, both of you."

We went and stood before her, hope lighting up our eyes like a rising sun.

"You really ain't got nobody in this world, either of you?"

We solemnly shook our heads.

"You two promise to be good and helpful, like you said?"

"Yes, ma'am."

"Oh, yes, ma'am!"

"Well, then, I guess you can start clearing off the table from the boarders. After breakfast is picked up and lunch on its way, we'll see about having you choose a room for yourselves."

"You mean we can stay?"

"Yes, heaven give me strength."

I leaned against the dry sink, beaming, but Mandy, she reached out and gave Mrs. Bergman a bodacious hug. Nobody could mistake her for anything but a girl with a display like that.

"Oh, you won't be sorry, ma'am. You truly won't be sorry! Jack and me, we'll be good as gold."

I smiled at the picture the two of them made, as I fingered the string around my neck.

Chapter 7

IT WAS WONDERFUL at Mrs. Bergman's boardinghouse. We put New York City, the Children's Aid Society, and that old orphan train out of our minds for the duration and set in to get acquainted with our obligations and the town.

That mean cold rain didn't last out the rest of our first day. It was spring that came in with glory, but we hardly noticed it, we was so busy. It took some doing, getting used to everything new. And after the first few days, when we got our morning chores sorted out, Mrs. Bergman actually let us go to school! Being on the streets and on the road as long as we had, there wasn't nothing that could compare to the settled feeling this gave Mandy and me.

The New Hope Grammar School was a right proper schoolhouse. It sat on a hill with a view of the river and everything a few blocks behind Mrs. Bergman's place, just over the Delaware Canal that snaked through behind her alley and up a few streets. The school had a bunch of rooms, because New Hope turned out bigger than we'd expected—near two hundred houses, counting those running off into side streets that we hadn't seen in the gloom of our first morning. It was painted up a nice bright white like the rest of the town. Mr. Edward Struthers, our boarder, he was Mandy's and my teacher. He had asthma and didn't have the strength to cane a body too hard. And he had a wondrous soft way of talking. Knew his business, too. He even taught me a few things about sums that I hadn't already figured out in my former business life. And long division and fractions, why, they was sheer revelations.

Mandy, she took more to the McGuffey's Readers than to the arithmetic, but I liked the Readers just fine, too, and after only a week I got graduated to McGuffey's Fifth Level. That introduced me to writers I'd never heard of, like Hawthorne and Longfellow and Irving. In under a week I'd read through that whole book before tucking in at night by the light of my kerosene lamp.

It also turned out useful that Mr. Struthers was a permanent boarder at our place. He seen right off that Mandy and me was keen on learning and loaned us some books from his private collection. He had all of Washington Irving's stuff and even a wondrous volume on the Old West, called *The Oregon Trail*, by a Mr. Parkman, who had actually hunted with Injuns when there was more of them around. And over his coffee after supper Mr. Struthers liked to tell stories about how George Washington himself had stayed in New Hope years back, during the Revolution, and even crossed the river in the middle of icy winter like we'd done. And to think that all took place just a few miles downriver at Taylorsville.

But getting back to the school proper, there was a bunch of other children studying there, too. About twenty-five of us in our class alone: some big, walloping fellows that come in from their farms each day when there was a lull in the plowing, and two of the five Richters, whose pa owned the general store and boating-supply establishment down the street from us, and the Justice of the Peace's daughter, and the blacksmith's boy twins, to name a few.

I'd only gone to school once before, back before the diphtheria struck. There weren't no comparison. That'd been a big-city school building, with upwards of seventy-five of us in each room, three to a desk, no windows for air, and a master who thrived on whippings. Hadn't been no deprivation to leave that place.

I guess I was learning to like New Hope just fine. And Mandy, why she was thriving. Her hair was growing out and Mrs. Bergman fixed up a couple of pretty dresses for her. But she still let Mandy wear her britches underneath, on cold days.

And our chores at the boardinghouse weren't no hardship. I chopped a little kindling and carted coal around some, and emptied out the ashes. I also washed a fair amount of dishes and pots and pans in scalding water each and every day. Then, once a week, Mandy and me set down and polished up all the lamp chimneys. Mrs. Bergman's girls used to hate to do that job, on account of it left them smudged all over. But Mandy and me, it just took us back to our bootblacking days, so we didn't mind a bit.

Laundry day was the hardest, but as spring came in balmier, it wasn't so bad hauling all that water around and banging at the sheets and such in the copper vats Mrs. Bergman had set up out back. Course, then, Mandy still had to give a hand at ironing up them linens with a big old mangle, and changing beds, but she did it smiling and singing. I never knew she could sing before.

So there we were, setting in fine after about a month. I figured over it all one day while out on an errand down to the general store after school. I was taking my usual roundabout way, just balancing on the edge of the canal behind our place, waving at an occasional barge hauling coal or whiskey down from Easton, then heading over toward the river to smell the sawdust at the New Hope Sawmill the town got named after. It felt good, poking an old barrel stave into interesting-looking holes, moseying along, not having to worry about where the next meal was coming from or where I was to set my head that night. It was a fine feeling. Freer than I'd expected. Because you know, deep down inside, I wasn't ever sure how well it'd work out at the boardinghouse. A fellow likes to have a little space around him, specially when he's been on his own so much. But Mrs. Bergman, she seemed to know just when to let me off to wander when I needed that space. She was a lot like Miss Blackman that way, understanding how I thought, without asking. I got so into considering all that stuff, I clean forgot to get the liniment for Mrs. Bergman's rheumatism, and had to double back to the store. I was that high on everything.

Come the first of May, you never seen anything as beautiful as Pennsylvania. The chickens was scratching in the new grass out behind the boardinghouse, and colorful weeds was sprouting all up and down the sides of the canal and South Main Street, the big road to the front of our house that we'd first hiked in on. When Mandy and I walked down to the edge of the Delaware, the soft, tree-covered rolling land to either side was the prettiest thing you could imagine. It beat the pants off of New York. So little grew there it was hard to tell the passing seasons aside from the heat or cold. I had to mention it to Mandy. We was standing there, admiring, she with a new bonnet tied on to keep the sun from her eyes.

"Ain't it something, all the fresh green! And the Delaware. Sure reminds me of the ocean, all that river water flowing so hard to get somewhere. Out to the sea, I guess."

"I never seen the ocean, Jack. Least I don't remember it. Pa mentioned once I was born atop it, though, in steerage, coming over from Ireland."

"I never knew you was born on the way."

"I was. And my ma, she died right after birthing me. It was in a storm, my pa said. He told me one time when he wasn't feeling really mean. It must have been between the second and third growler of the evening. That was usually his nicest moment." She shook her head, as if trying to lose the sudden picture in it. "Now, that must be the first time I remembered my pa since we got here. Who do you suppose is running for his beer now?"

"I don't rightly guess it matters anymore."

"You're right, Jack. It doesn't. Let's go explore down by the covered bridge. It's the closest I'll probably ever get to the ocean. Mrs. Bergman said we didn't have to help with supper today. She said to get some fresh air."

Mandy was already running down the bank, pulling me after her. We skidded to the water's edge and chose stones to practice throwing as far as we could. Someday I figured on getting one of mine clean across that Delaware.

"How did you get to see the ocean?"

"Old Fred Huffmaier made a special-order wedding cake one time for a German family out on Long Island. I got to ride with the delivery boy to make certain it wouldn't get too banged up on the way. It took all day to get there and back. It was a powerful sight, that ocean."

"I like this, too. And the mountains starting up over to the west."

"The Poconos, I guess, that Mr. Struthers mentioned. He said rich folks go there for summering. They're supposed to have some real fine waterfalls. We might be seeing some of them in another month. The rich folks, that is. Mrs. Bergman said as how a few lodge with her now and again, then go out hiking from here."

Mandy laughed. "Can you imagine hiking just for the fun of it, Jack? After all that walking we did to get here, I don't want to think about ever doing any more. How could a person just up and leave their homes like that, anyway?"

"Well, maybe if they're solid secure in them, it don't make no difference. They know there'll be a place to come back to."

"I don't think I'll ever feel that way, Jack. Sure enough to leave, I mean."

"We ain't been settled down long enough yet, Mandy. Maybe this time next year you'll feel different."

"Maybe."

I grabbed Mandy by the arm. "Enough of this silly stuff. Let's play hide-an'-seek. You're it!" And I took off for the covered toll bridge down the shore so fast she didn't know what had become of me.

School let out for the summer toward the end of May. That was mostly so the farmers' children could help out with the work full-time. Mr. Struthers seemed relieved. I noticed when I walked home from school with him on one of the last days. There was a new kind of springiness to his steps, as if he was looking forward to something special. Turned out it was rocks. We were almost down to the canal when he opened up about them, like he didn't get too many people to talk to about the subject.

"Only another week, Jack, and I'll be on my way to the Chesapeake Bay in Maryland to go fossil hunting for the holidays."

"No offense, sir, but I never heard tell of a 'fossil.' What's it do?"

He actually smiled. "They're rocks, Jack, but special ones. The long-dead bones of ancient animals, and the imprints of plants. Most of them are millions of years old. If my luck is good, I'll bring you a specimen for your own. Or at least a few sharks' teeth. There are always plenty of them around." His eyes were gazing off into the distance now, but they weren't looking at anything in New Hope. "If only my health were more stable, I would prefer a trip out West, to where the really big fossils are." Then he seemed to remember something and was back again, looking at me. "See that you look after Mrs. Bergman in my absence, young man. She still gets bad bouts of the malarial ague from her days out West."

I didn't see how Mrs. Bergman had suddenly gotten into the conversation, but nodded agreement and proceeded to forget about the whole thing. It was too nice a day to be worrying over people's health. This fossil business was more interesting. I'd have to remember to tell Mandy about it. But it didn't make much sense they could be millions of years old, like Mr. Struthers said. Why, according to Reverend Quilley's last sermon down the street at Mrs. Bergman's church, it had only taken the Lord seven days to make the world, and it warn't much more than three or four thousand years old now, at best.

I hit Mr. Struthers with that one right then and there, by the little bridge over the canal.

He got a curious look on his face. "I'll have to give you Darwin's *Origin of Species* to read in the fall, Jack, when you've grown a few more brain cells. You just may be ready for the theory of evolution by then."

I was fixing to ask him what brain cells were, and evolution, too, but by that time we'd gotten back to Mrs. Bergman's and Mr. Struthers took off in a hurry to begin his packing.

He left a few days later, not more than an hour after school had been dismissed for the final time. He sure was in a hurry to clear out from under all his students. Mandy and me helped carry his bags to the waiting buggy he'd rented. You could see he was all over excitement—least as excited as he ever let on to being—and was itching to leave.

We waited while he climbed in the buggy and stopped to blow his nose into a big handkerchief he always carried with him. I never saw anybody like him for having a cold all year round that way.

Then Mr. Struthers looks down at Mandy and me from the buggy. "You remember what we were talking about the other day, Jack. Between you and Mandy and Mary and Agnes, there's no reason Mrs. Bergman has to wear herself out like she does."

"I'll make sure and pass that on to Mary and Agnes."

Mr. Struthers just smiled that rare gentle smile that always lit up his skinny face. He knew as well as Mandy and me that those local girls stop work and start in on gossiping the minute Mrs. Bergman's out of sight. Sometimes she's just too tenderhearted. But there ain't too many servant girls to be had around here, so I guess she was also trying to make the best of what was available.

Mr. Struthers gave me one more look. "Jack, you may also tell Mrs. Bergman you have my permission to go into my room. I've just graduated you to Sir Walter Scott. Start with *Ivanhoe*. If you encounter any difficult words, use my Webster's Dictionary, the way I taught you. See you at the end of summer!"

We watched the schoolmaster till the dust kicked up by the buggy was settled down and he out of sight. Then I raced for his room.

I got *Ivanhoe* finished all right, but never got to move beyond that. Mrs. Bergman's ague had begun kicking up, as promised. And her rheumatism, too, so she was spending more time in bed than out. I couldn't understand it.

The rheumatism should of been better now that the cold weather was past.

But there was a couple of seed and farm-equipment drummers staying with us, keeping us too busy to worry much over it, and a new one trying to sell corsets to Bo Richter. I was down to the general store when Smedley the corset man gave his spiel.

"It's only good sense to stock in Good Sense Corset Waists, Mr. Richter. Look here." He pulled one out of his traveling case and held it up. "Fits all ages, from infants to adults. It's even got a patent-pending ring buckle at the hip for hose supporters. It's got tape-fastened buttons that won't pull off! It's got cord-edged buttonholes that won't wear out! Nothing but the best materials used throughout, Mr. Richter. Every woman and mother in town will want them."

Bo Richter, he just stood there, slowly shaking his head no. "Won't do, Smedley. Women got too much work to do to be tied up in one of them newfangled things. How they supposed to bend over their washing tubs with one of them holding them in?" He looked at it again. "And I wouldn't put one of them on my little Emmeline and Rachel if you paid me. It'd stunt their growth, it would, by the looks of it."

"Mr. Richter! How could you think such a thing? Why *thousands* of Good Sense Corsets are now being worn all over these United States. They're the height of fashion. Women *like* fashion, Mr. Richter. And as for health, why there ain't nothing more comfortable than one of these things. It reorganizes the body in the proper mode for healthful breathing."

"How would you know? You ever tried on one of them contraptions?"

Smedley, he looked pained. But it weren't a bad idea on Mr. Richter's part. It might've held together Smedley's potbelly some. It might've even squeezed some of his neck hair up to cover that bald spot on top of his head.

I got to snickering at the thought, and Mr. Richter looked at me. "What do you think, Jack? Would you put Mandy in one these newfangled chest traps?"

That stopped me short. "Over my dead body," said I.

"I thought so. Off with you now, Mr. Smedley. I'm a busy man, as you can see."

He weren't particularly at that moment, there being a lull in anything happening at all. Smedley seemed to notice it, too, and was about to remark on the fact, when Mr. Richter finished up. "Seems to me you better head on down the river, Mr. Smedley. All the way to Philadelphia. Them city ladies ain't got nothing better to set their attention on. Maybe they'll buy a few off of you." Mr. Richter stopped then, like Smedley's not even in the store anymore. "How's Mrs. Bergman feeling today, Jack?"

"That's what I come for, Mr. Richter. You got any more of that Lydia Pinkham's Vegetable Compound we tried last week? It seemed to give her some comfort."

"I got a fresh case just the other day. Here you go, boy."

Smedley left the next morning, but not until after I caught him locked up in the pantry with Agnes when I was looking for a fresh jar of pickled corn relish to set on the table. You'd think she'd have a little better sense

112

than that. The seed drummer was much better-looking. But I guess the seed drummer didn't have no corsets.

Agnes wore Smedley's for three whole days after he left, walking around the complete time like she was in deep agony. After that, I seen it stuffed underneath the bucket of ashes I hauled out of the kitchen. I just buried it in the ash pile and didn't say nothing more about it.

Mrs. Bergman wasn't getting any better, even with her constant swigging of Lydia Pinkham's. The fact was, one day in early June I looked on her propped up on her pillows in her bed and hardly recognized her. She didn't have that comfortable plump look anymore. It had just disappeared when I wasn't paying much attention. Her skin hung down now, all over. It made me sad. She didn't even seem to have the strength to grab on to her knitting needles. Her ball of wool just sat there on the covers in front of her.

I had to cheer her up somehow. "Did Mandy tell you about the new additions?"

"No, dear. What do you mean?"

"Old Henrietta out back, she finally hatched her eggs we been letting her set on. All sixteen of 'em come out chirping. Then Charles, he sees them chicks lined up behind his wife and lets out such a crowing and flapping of wings it could of brung the sun up again."

Mrs. Bergman tried a chuckle, but I could see it hurt. "You'd better bring me a cup of that camomile tea, Jack dear. And bring Mandy with it. I need to talk to the two of you."

I shook my head. If that silly rooster Charles couldn't

get a rise out of Mrs. Bergman, she was really in a bad way. So I went for Mandy. She was fixing up a big pile of early garden flowers in an empty pickle jar for Mrs. Bergman's room.

"Don't they look sweet, Jack?"

I was busy pouring the hot water always left on the hob. "Fine, Mandy. Just fine."

She looked at me. "What's the matter, Jack?"

"Mrs. Bergman's worse today. She wants to talk to both of us."

Her fingers stopped arranging. "She's going to die on us, isn't she, Jack? I've been praying and praying that she won't, but I don't think the Lord is paying me any mind." She looked up at me. "What we really need is a priest, Jack. A real, good priest with Holy Communion and such. But they haven't got one in New Hope yet, even with all these people. Only Reverend Quilley at the Baptist church, and he's not the same at all. The Methodist and Presbyterian ministers, neither. They've got a priest upriver in Frenchtown, though, Agnes was saying. Maybe we ought to go after him."

"What we really need is a doctor, Mandy. But maybe one of them wouldn't even help. He'd probably just bleed her and leave her sicker than before. Maybe that's why she refuses to see Doc Hopkins." I was beginning to feel worse the more I thought about it. "Why do the best people have to get sick and old?"

Mandy didn't have an answer to that any more than I had. So we took the camomile tea up to Mrs. Bergman's room. She had us sit on the edge of her bed, managed a sip from her cup, then almost spilled it from trembling fingers. I caught it quiet-like, and balanced it on my knees.

"You see this quilt, Mandy?" The old woman's voice was soft as she said it.

Mandy nodded faintly, a worried look in her eye.

"I want this to be yours. You always admired the flower design and the colors. The pattern's called Prairie Flower. I made it myself, the first winter I spent on the plains with Mr. Bergman, after he married me fresh out of New Hope. I guess I could have picked the Rocky Road to Kansas pattern instead, considering the trip and how we lived. It was in a dugout in Kansas. It was too cold for most anything else but quilting." Her eyes were faraway now, looking back on that time.

"We were still newlyweds, and not another soul to talk to for miles. It was always damp in that house. We couldn't seem to get the damp out of it noway. And just the great pile of buffalo chips to warm us while the wind blowed for days, burying and unburying us with drifts of snow. I thought we'd never survive it. We weren't ever so close again." The faded blue of her eyes snapped back to us, that old time buried again. "By rights it should go to my daughter, but it never took Eldora the same way."

Mandy was trying hard not to sniffle now, and Mrs. Bergman made believe she didn't see.

"Jack, put out your hand."

I did, while she fiddled in the drawer of the little table next to her bedstead. Then I felt something flat and cool, with round edges, slip onto my palm. I closed my fingers around it, afraid to look.

"That was my husband's watch. It should go to my son Elbert, but he's got two or three watches of his own by this time. He went up to Minneapolis, from Kansas, you know. He's got his own little business up there, and doing just fine with it."

She lay back against her pillows, hard, like she was just about used up. But there was still something she wanted to say.

"I wanted both of you to have something from me. I even wrote it up in letters I sent to my children, so they wouldn't try to take them away from you after, or accuse you of stealing them. I wanted them to know you were both good children. Good as gold, just like you promised. I asked them to see for you, too, but who knows what will come of that. Don't be putting too much stock in it. Elbert and Eldora, they're mighty busy people now. And they live so far away. They'll probably never even see me buried here back East. I don't even know why I came back. Except home didn't feel like home anymore out in Kansas without Mr. Bergman."

I sat there holding her cup and the watch, feeling mighty low, but understanding what she was saying, too. That's about how I'd have felt without Mandy. It all pained too much to dwell on.

"There ain't no need for you to be giving up things, Mrs. Bergman. Another couple of weeks and we'll have you out back pounding at the wash again."

"Well, that, at least, is something I won't miss! I'm quite sure I won't be needing to do laundry where I hope to go. I figure Mr. Bergman will be waiting for me. He's had enough time by now to build us a little house up there. It oughtn't be cold, like our first winter, but I wouldn't mind if it were. No, I wouldn't mind at all."

Mrs. Bergman died two days later. Bo Richter harnessed up his rig and drove over to the next town to fetch a coffin and undertaker for the burying. They laid her in the cemetery on the hill behind the Bible Baptist church. It was too bad Mr. Bergman wasn't next to her but still off in Kansas. It seemed kind of lonely for her there that way. Mandy and me, we were right up front by the grave, with most of the town around us. I tried to get some comfort out of the watch in my pocket, but it was the key around my neck that I ended up hanging on to. It hadn't brought neither me nor Mandy to the right door yet.

The Bergman children, they arrived a week after that. To be fair, they seemed sorry to have missed the funeral, but they was in an almighty hurry to close down the boardinghouse and settle all the rest of Mrs. Bergman's affairs. They boxed up Mr. Struthers' books, kicked out the two old maids and the old gent with no teeth, boarded up the windows and put a "For Sale" sign up front before they properly took the time to look at Mandy and me. And even then they didn't look too long.

When they finally decided to take some notice of us, Elbert, he looks at Eldora. "How much room you got at your place in Omaha, Dora?" he says.

"Not enough," she says.

"I figured. The boy I could maybe use in my business, but it's going through a depression right now. I don't expect it to last too long, mind you, but in the meantime he'd be eating up profits, so to speak."

"The girl's too young yet to be trained as a proper servant, Bert, although she might be some use to look after the baby."

The both of them were talking this way right in front of Mandy and me, like we wasn't even there. It made us feel pretty bad. And it for certain sure didn't make us hunger after going with either of them two. How that nice Mrs. Bergman could of ended up with such children was beyond my understanding. I could see now why she give us that watch and quilt. I felt for the watch in my pocket. Its gold was still nice and cool, even in the heat of the summer day. Cold watch and warm quilt. Like that good winter Mrs. Bergman had spent in the dugout.

"You needn't bother about us none," I said then. "Mandy and me, we'll make out. We always do. We'll just stay here in New Hope."

Well, they acted like I hadn't said nothing. I guess I was beneath their notice. They just went right on figuring.

"The nearest orphanage is probably in Philadelphia, and neither of us have the time to fetch them down there. They'd be put to better use with one of the farmers around here. They're not too young, either of them, to help out with that kind of work."

"You always were good with ideas, Bert. We'll take them to Sunday service this morning. We'll have Reverend Quilley ask for homes."

They did, too.

Chapter 8

I WOULDN'T WANT to go through that morning in church again. We was hauled up next to the pulpit and showed off like prize livestock. Course, we was bigger and healthier-looking after our time with Mrs. Bergman, so I, for one, didn't feel too runty, but it was still bad. After the good times at the boardinghouse, I felt like I was about to go through one of them depressions like Elbert had talked about. What come was worse.

Reverend Quilley gave a talk about Christian charity, and community duty, and looking after the least among us—the least being Mandy and me, I guessed. I wished Mr. Struthers had been around rather than off gallivanting amongst his dead bones. There weren't no one in the entire congregation I felt I could trust. It hadn't done no good mentioning it to Elbert and Eldora, but I still felt like shouting out that Mandy and I would rather be together, on our own, than just anybody's apprenticed servants. Mrs. Bergman had made us a little picky about our futures. But these grownups was so wrapped up in their Christian duties to what they considered helpless orphans that I was sure not a one would listen. Bo Richter might of been all right, at least to talk it over with, but he belonged to the Methodists, and had five youngsters of his own already anyhow. It appeared that righteousness might be our undoing again.

Also, I was never set on being the absolute center of attention. It was one thing back in New York trying to drum up business with the papers or the blacking kit, trying to catch a few eyes. But standing up here by the pulpit all this time while Reverend Quilley rambled on, well, I felt like every one of them eyes in the congregation was on me—and Mandy, hanging on to me for dear life to one side.

A few of the farmer types had gotten out of their pews and come up to stand just below the pulpit, about three feet lower than us. And I could see their women behind them, looking, nudging their spouses, pointing at one or t'other of us. Reverend Quilley thought he'd almost got us out of his hair now and was beaming, as jovial as his dour face would allow.

"There's nothing either of these children need but three square meals a day to make them welcome, useful additions to any of your homes," the Reverend continued with his sales pitch. "Take young Jack McConnell here, for instance. How old are you, my lad?"

"I'm eleven near as I can figure, but I ain't your lad, and wouldn't never be, neither. Sir." I added in the "Sir" because Mrs. Bergman would expect a little respect shown to my elders. But it was true enough about the rest. Living with a total diet of hell and damnation didn't appeal to me nohow.

Reverend Quilley, he looks kind of pained for a long

moment, then tries to make the best of it. "You see? The boy has natural wit. A sure sign of a good mind. Which amongst you would like to take a closer look at young Jack?"

Two of the men jumped up off the main floor and commenced to poke at me. One grunted and jumped down again, but the other, he opened my mouth to inspect my teeth. I chomped down. Mandy gave me a fearful look and pulled at me, as if I were going about this business entirely the wrong way. Maybe she was right, but my dander was up.

"Think it's a horse I am? My choppers are as good as anybody else's, and there's the proof for it."

The Reverend Quilley looked like he was ready to go into a fit, but a third farmer, down below, spoke up. "Truth to say, the boy's got a good bite. There may be some strength of character present. And there's enough work at my place to exorcise the serpent that bites out of him. We'll take him."

They did. Felix and Essie Swopes and their boys Clifford and Amos stood for me. I knew Clifford and Amos. They was two of those strapping big galoots that come to school from time to time, but they was in the oldest class. I also recognized them from dropping off Mrs. Bergman's fresh milk on Saturdays. Their pa generally made the other weekday deliveries during the winter. They had a farm two or three miles out of town, the usual hundred acres, with cows and such.

But the worst was Mandy being taken right after me by another family, the Petersons. Their place was ten miles beyond the Swopes'. I'd never seen any of them Petersons at school, and figured there weren't no way Mandy'd get into town for classes come September, even in good weather. There weren't much chance of us seeing each other, neither, except maybe once in a while for the Sunday service. But the Petersons didn't always make it in for those Sundays. I didn't know much else about the Petersons, except they had a passel of peaked, glum-looking youngsters. I wasn't sure what they wanted with another mouth to feed.

Neither the Petersons nor the Swopes give us much time for our goodbyes. Right after the service, they hauled their buggies up to the boardinghouse and waited while we went to get our things. We shoved our stuff into our old knapsacks, the both of us sniffling from our different sides of the room. I threw my books in last, then on sudden thought hauled out the dream book and gave it to Mandy.

She looked at it, then started in bawling out loud.

"I . . . I can't take the dream book, Jack!"

"Why not?"

"It's *ours*. It belongs to both of us. We bought it together, on money we made from the papers and boots."

"Well, I know that, Mandy. I want you to have it anyway. On loan. Till we get together again."

"When will that be?"

I jerked out my handkerchief and poked it at her. "They're yelling for us out front. Dry up your face. I'll come visit you soon as I can. Even if I have to steal a horse to do it."

"I know you will, Jack. But—"

Then there wasn't any more time. Clifford Swopes was

at the bedroom door. "What's keeping you two? Oh-ho. Hey, Amos! They're in here, crying like babies!"

Well, I went to fetch Clifford a good punch, but Mandy stopped me. "He's way bigger than you, Jack," she whispered. "Let's just go now."

And she wiped her face and gave me back the handkerchief and we marched out. I got to sit in the back of the Swopes' wagon, next to my pack, while Clifford and Amos rode alongside on their private mounts. At last view, Mrs. Bergman's boardinghouse looked lonesomer than even me, all closed up the way it was. Like it was hiding its eyes in sorrow.

The Swopes' house wasn't anything to brag about. Not after Mrs. Bergman's. They'd put up a little two-story frame farmhouse. And the animals were sheltered in a run-down barn surrounded by rickety sheds that sort of leaned into all the rocky hills starting up on their land. Giving the spread a quick look, it seemed to me like all the comfort and richness of New Hope and the surrounding hills had just passed this hundred acres by. It was all moderately clean, but the flies were something else. They was everywhere.

The Swopes, they gave me a place to sleep up in the attic. It was the hottest part of the place in the summer. Probably the coldest in winter, too. And the roof was so low there wasn't anywhere I could stand up straight without banging my head. But at least I didn't have to share with Clifford and Amos.

That first night I lay there on the corn-shuck mattress they gave me for the floor. That's all they gave me. A prickly corn-shuck mattress stitched up with scratchy old burlap, a blanket, and a can for a chamber pot. Not even a candle or lamp.

I got to feeling sorry for myself right off. Then I stopped and considered. What was I fussing about? This here corn-shuck mattress and blanket and pot were more than anybody ever gave me in New York. Not to mention a roof over my head and vittles. I guessed that short spell at Mrs. Bergman's must of spoiled me something terrible. Here I was, suddenly expecting something for nothing, instead of going out and looking after my own interests like I'd done for so long.

I decided then and there that I'd do my best for the Swopes, the best that they'd let me. They wouldn't of been my first family choice, but I figured if Clifford and Amos could live with me, I'd do my best to put up with them.

Then I went back to finishing my inventory of the place, like Bo Richter was always doing at his general store. There wasn't but one window, and after they closed the trapdoor on me, I pulled my mattress over to it and got the window open so I could breathe. That was a mistake, 'cause the flies came buzzing in like they'd been waiting, just knowing I was in there. Then I had to decide, was it better to fight off flies all night or choke to death on the stale hot air. I chose the flies, but didn't I wish I had one of them cigar butts from New York with me. I could of lit it up and the wicked smoke would of had them flies all dead and gone in no time.

The next morning was Monday and I got to know the schedule of the Swopes right quick. Up before daybreak to milk the cows. And it wasn't even just before daybreak. It was more like bakery hours, three or four of the morning.

About those cows. They seemed even bigger than the ones Mandy and I had decided against trying to milk that first night in the barn out from Jersey City. I still wasn't keen on hanging on to their privates to squeeze out the milk. Amos, who'd sat me down on a stool in front of one, he sees me looking kind of squeamish and pokes Clifford with his elbow, hard.

"Jist lookit that city boy, Cliff. He ain't never had an udder in his hand afore! Don't know what to do with it!"

Then they both set in to laughing their fool heads off.

That brought Mr. Swopes. "What in tarnation is this nonsense about?" He looked at me sitting there on the three-legged stool, not knowing what to do with myself.

" 'Take my yoke upon you and learn from me.' " He was always quoting bits out of the Bible like that. He bent down and gave me a brief demonstration. "You pull 'em, boy. One after the other. And you don't lose no milk. 'Let nothing be wasted.' We be needing it for our milk runs, not to mention the cheeses and the hogs."

Well, he stood there like he was daring me, Clifford and Amos off to the rear, still poking at each other, giggling behind his back. So I pulled. The first lick must've been way too hard with all that pressure I was feeling, 'cause that cow let out a moan and tried to kick me out of the barn. There was more laughing and back slapping, and I got the knack of it after that. But the prospect of going on down the line and doing the same to another dozen of these beasts, twice a day, didn't have much appeal for me.

Then there was the chickens to feed soon as they got off their roosts. And the hogs to swill. Vicious hogs that would as soon eat me as the food I set before them. Then go in to breakfast. Mrs. Swopes fixed a nice table, but by the time the Bible was took out, and then the praying done, the vittles was all covered with flies and me not wanting to put it in my mouth anymore.

After breakfast the two boys loaded up the wagon with milk cans and went off for their summer deliveries to New Hope. They'd be gone till noon. As for the rest of the farm, it was divided up into either pasturage or fields of alfalfa and corn for winter fodder. They was already planted, so there wasn't much to be done with them except pray for rain, or pray for sun, whichever seemed more useful at the moment. The Swopes done this serious-like every evening.

There was also the vegetable garden. That was given to me, in order that Clifford and Amos could take more time fooling with their horses afternoons. There was a lot of talk about raising Standardbreds, and they was saving their money to buy up another mare. For dairy farmers, they sure was crazy about horses. It was the only soft thing I could find in them, save for the paunches around their middles.

They had two big horses—part Clydesdales, they said—for the team work on the farm and hauling the milk; then they had another couple more. Two were Standardbred mares, and Amos and Clifford's private mounts. The third was a young stud they'd just bought for the breeding. This stud hadn't ever been ridden, or even driven, and was still pretty wild. They also talked a lot about the autumn races at the county fair, like they was getting set to raise some entries for the trotting.

I'd been listening to the farmers that hung around Bo Richter's store when they come into town, and had picked up a thing or two about local methods. So it seemed to me that maybe the Swopes had a few horses too many to be fed all winter from their patchy land, and nowheres near enough pasturage or cleverness for raising up and training a good racing horse. Still, it wasn't any of my business. I just hoed and weeded through the heat of the day, up till milking time again, when the cows needed to be herded in and the milk carried down to the spring-house for cooling till morning.

After there wasn't any more garden work to be done, I was set to polishing harness, and even painting up the outside of the house. It was a gray, raw-boarded house when I arrived, but pretty soon it turned a nice white. Those boards sure lapped up the paint, though, like they'd just been waiting on me to do the job.

Well, all that took time to get used to, but after the first two nights in that attic I smartened up some and began sneaking out of the house at bedtime. Those Swopes, they could sure sleep. After dinner and the Bible reading, they just fell into their beds like the dead. And soon as I heard their snores vibrating through the whole house, I just eased up the trapdoor so it didn't creak, and let myself down the attic ladder and past the two second-story bedrooms and out of the house into the fields. I fetched along the wool blanket Mrs. Swopes gave me, like it was December already, and laid it out in a nice spot I found in the alfalfa, near to the little crick that gurgled through the springhouse. Not too close in to the house so they could see where I'd probably ruined a few yards of their precious hay, but close enough so's I could hear them clattering out to the cows in the morning and act like I was just using the fields instead of the outhouse before milking.

It was nice, lying under the moon and stars like that. Much cooler than in the house, and hardly any flies to get at me. I was always pretty tired by that time, but it felt good to have a piece of the day to myself, private. I'd think about New York, and the trip, and wonder how Miss Blackman was doing. But especially I'd think about Mandy.

Once in a while I'd take out a lantern and one of my books. I'd read through *Snow-Bound* time and again, picturing Mandy and me, together, wrapped up in the snug cocoon of that snowed-in home. After about three weeks, I just couldn't stand thinking about her anymore. I missed her so bad I had to do something about seeing her. I thought and thought on it. Finally I decided if she didn't show at the church meeting come the next Sunday I'd have to take matters in my own hands, even if it really meant stealing one of the Swopes boys' horses, which I couldn't ride and was scared to death of anyway. Those horses seemed to have a wild streak in them, just like Clifford and Amos. Mean wild.

Sunday-go-to-meeting came and we all got dressed in our clean set of clothes and got in the buggy for town. I'd taken special care to wash and try to comb down my hair, wanting to look nice for Mandy. Shouldn't have taken the trouble. It hadn't rained for at least a week, and by the time we pulled into New Hope, I must've been covered with three inches of road dust that spilled over me in the back of that wagon. But I jumped down and dusted myself off best I could, then looked around hopeful-like for the Petersons.

I was still looking all through Reverend Quilley's sermon. I must of spent the better part of three hours craning my neck toward the door behind us. It didn't do no good. Mandy never came. Worse, some of the town fellows rushed up to me after service and wanted to know was we staying for covered-dish dinner. I knew right off I was sunk. Mrs. Swopes hadn't brought no covered dish along.

I lay awake half that night under the stars, thinking things out, and come Monday morning, I had a plan. But first I'd ask to be allowed to see Mandy, even though I didn't put much hope in that happening. I'd start with Mrs. Swopes. She tried to be kind, but was always so tired from the cooking and the washing and her other chores, not to mention being near scared to death of her husband. I'd do it early, whilst I was bringing in the milk. She'd maybe be less weary then.

I put the bucket down real easy on the floor next to where she was standing, her gingham shirtwaist sleeves rolled up past her elbows, kneading dough for the day's baking.

"Morning, Mrs. Swopes."

She jumped away from her breadboard like I'd bit her. "Is that you, Jack? You gave me a start, coming in so quiet. You can always hear Clifford and Amos near a mile off."

"I guess that's 'cause they're bigger, ma'am."

She gave her lump of dough a few more good thumps with arms not fat but thick with muscles like a strongman I'd seen once when Barnum's Circus came through New York. Her whole body was like that, honed down to hard muscle. Her husband and the boys tended more to big bones and pudginess. It made me wonder what she had to fear from them. She could of took them all in a fair fight.

"You swill the hogs, Jack?"

"Yes, ma'am."

"And took care of the chickens, too?"

"Yes, ma'am."

Then I sort of stood around, balancing on one foot, not sure how to broach Mandy.

"Something you want, Jack? You seem to be doing pretty good here. You getting enough to eat?"

"Yes, ma'am. No complaints there, ma'am. You're a fine cook."

Finally she let go of that lump and eyed me. "What is it, then, boy?"

"It's about my 'dopted sister, ma'am. The one that the Petersons took?"

She waited.

I finally let it out. "I miss her something terrible, ma'am. If I could just go to visit with her, maybe regular-like. Once a week? I wouldn't mind walking the ten miles. Not at all."

That must have broke the spell, because she started in attacking the floury mess again. "I had a favorite sister once. Ain't seen her since I married Mr. Swopes. And she not more than fifty miles to the other side of Philadelphia. Mr. Swopes don't go in for visiting nor gossiping. He just says the Lord made us to sweat and strive upon this earthly vale of tears."

"I guess that's why you don't stay for the church potlucks. But seems to me you'd work with a more cheerful heart if you got a chance to do a little socializing now and again."

"That was my thought fifteen years ago, boy. But the best I could do was make Swopes promise to let the boys ride off to school now and again. I can't see him giving you a full day off to walk ten miles over to the Petersons' and back again nohow. Especially not now that he's got you so trained to the work. If I was you, I'd just get that girl out of your mind. And I sure wouldn't mention nothing about it to my husband. It might just start him off. He's a fair man most of the time, but once in a blue moon something sets him off and he's more like a rampaging bull."

Then she stopped and covered up her loaves for raising. It was the most I'd ever heard her speak at one time. It seemed to answer my question fair and square, with a no, just like I'd figured.

I began edging out of the kitchen. "Thank you anyway, ma'am. I'm sure sorry about your sister."

She looked up at that reminder and I think I maybe saw a little look of sorrow in her eyes. Then it was gone.

"That's finished. Everything's finished. There's just the bread to make, and then the stove to keep going for the three everlasting meals. And the clothes to wash and mend. Ain't nothing else left for me in this life, and no future in thinking otherwise."

I paused at the door. "The house does look nicer painted up, doesn't it?"

"Don't hardly matter nohow. Ain't nobody going to come admiring it. I guess it'll help preserve the wood some, though."

Well, that put me straight on how things were at the Swopes place. And here I'd been thinking about maybe asking Mr. Swopes to make shutters for the windows so's I could paint them up a nice bright color. Red, maybe, like some of the barns was painted hereabouts. I knew from studying the shelves at Bo Richter's that it wasn't even dear to buy. Fact is, red ocher was the cheapest paint you could get. And the brightness of it put me in mind of some of the firehouse rigs in New York City.

It had even crossed my mind that he might like to pick up a few packets of flower seeds from Richter's next time he was in town with the milk. They'd look pretty planted up around the house, like at Mrs. Bergman's. Mandy had always took care of them flowers is what brought that thought to my mind. There weren't any flowers around the Swopes place, only the mistakes. And those mistakes, the weeds around the corn—bachelor buttons, and such— they was all plucked out like they was forerunners of the plague. There might have been a reason for that, but who knows? I guess I just didn't have the proper thinking necessary for a real farmer.

I shook all those thoughts from my mind, same as Mrs. Swopes had got rid of her favorite sister. But there wasn't no way I could do that about Mandy. A month without her was long enough. Fifteen years seemed closer to eternity. I'd have to go back to my plan.

It was a simple plan. First thing, I'd have to take an interest in the horses. That meant I had to take an interest in Clifford and Amos. The house was painted, and the harness never looked better, so I figured there had to be some time available for me to do all this. And a horse they'd let me near.

The horse part was the hardest. The only one available would be the new stud neither of them could get a handle on. It was a roan, which I gathered was rare for the breed, and it always had that look in its eye like it knew of better places it could be. I guess I knew what it was thinking, all right. So I figured, maybe this horse and I got more in common than would appear obvious. If I could get near him, maybe we could palaver some and come up with a mutually agreeable arrangement.

Then again, onct I got near him, I'd have to know what to do next. So that Monday after my talk with Mrs. Swopes, and after all the chores were done, I sidled up to Clifford and Amos down to the barn.

"Well, look who's here, Amos. It's our Jack. Got the harness all shined up, Jack?"

"You know I do."

"What about the house?"

"You can see for yourself it's as white as it can get. Also, there's no more paint."

"What about the garden, then?" threw in Amos.

"Your pa says I shouldn't fuss with it anymore. It's up to God now."

"Well, then, what are you fixing to do next, Jack?"

"Thought if you'd teach me to saddle up I could do that for you and Amos."

Well, they looked at each other like I was trying to play them some kind of trick. Maybe they wasn't as dumb as they acted. Then again, maybe they was.

Clifford winked at Amos. "You like the idea of havin' our own stable boy, Amos, like the rich swells at the races?"

"Don't they call them grooms? What do they do besides shovel out the manure, which our Jack already takes care of?"

"Why, in the homes of the e-lite, they groom the horses just so, saddle 'em up, and sometimes even help the rider mount."

"Well, I guess I can mount my own horse every time. Ain't no fine lady with a sidesaddle." Amos, he stood there chewing on a blade of grass, considering further. "Still, in this weather, would save a body a considerable amount of effort, not having to pick the hooves and do the grooming."

"Not to mention cooling the horse off after a good workout, eh, Amos?"

Clifford, he grinned at Amos, and the two look like they're about to put one over on me.

"Well, then," I said, "if you're agreeable, I'm set to learn. How about we start with the bit and bridle business."

By day, those two worked me hard, lording it over me something awful. But they did know a thing or two about horses. I was learning a thing or two as well. Right off, I got the point about being firm with the beasts, showing them who's master. But it seemed to me there might be something to be said for a little kindness as well. I worked on that theory by night.

The carrots were starting to come up in the garden from all the rains earlier on. In fact, they were coming in so well I figured a little weeding wouldn't hurt them none. Every night on my way out to sleep, I pulled up the biggest I could find, then trotted over to the paddock that was built out from the barn. In fair weather they always left the stallion in there so's he wouldn't get into mischief up in the pasture with the other horses. He would be standing off in one corner, separated by a fence from the dozing cows. The first few nights, he tried not to pay me any mind, and I had to eat the carrots myself. But he stood there watching, listening to me crunch as loud as I was able, showing him what he was missing.

After that, he started coming over and pulling the whole root from my hand. I'd sit on the fence then and talk to him, low and long. Like I was discussing the day with Mandy. He'd stay a few yards off, but I could tell he was listening. He was reddish-brown, with a thick sprinkling of white. Some of the white stood out in almost definite patches, making him easier to see by night. I liked to make believe he was a wild mustang from out West, and the two of us was living there, free as anything. It got so I almost had myself convinced he was more piebald than roan. That's how I come to give him his name, Carrot Pie.

After about two weeks, he was taking chunks of the carrot out of my hand, nuzzling my palm soft. He even let me pat his head. Next I came with two carrots and a bit just attached to two pieces of rope. I gave Pie the carrot, then slipped the bit in quick, between the grinding of his flat teeth. First he thought it was another carrot, then figured out it didn't taste anything as good. It took me two nights to get him back after that trick.

By the middle of August, I had him taking bit and bridle, and me as well, bareback. He didn't mind me on his back, but couldn't abide a saddle. Well, then, I thought, we'll just make do without the saddle. We'd leave for Mandy's the next night.

Now, all this time, it hadn't rained a whole lot. The fields were starting to dry out and we were needing another good burst mighty soon so's the corn wouldn't be stunted. The sky had been doing a fair amount of fireworks, though. I should know, because night after night I lay out under it, watching the heat lightning. Nothing ever come of it. So I didn't think nothing more about it when the night came I decided Pie and I were ready to visit Mandy and it started in with the heat flashes again. I just let Pie out of the pen, real quiet, then led him a ways off before mounting. I didn't want to take any chance of waking the Swopes. Then we rode off toward the Petersons', those lightning flashes acting like lanterns from God to show us the way.

Chapter 9

I HAD A FAIR idea of where the Petersons lived. I'd got it out of the Porter boys at the last church meeting, when I got permission to leave for a call of nature. The Porter boys had heard the same call and they and a bunch of non-Baptists were out back, playing marbles next to some of the parked buggies and wagons. I got down on my knees in the dust and watched the game of ringer for a while, wishing I could join in. Jim Porter must of read my mind, because he gave me a marble on loan, and let me use his shooter. I used to be pretty good back in New York, and before I judged it time to go back to the heat and fan-waving of the never-ending sermon, I won ten beauties, one of 'em a green cat's-eye. Jim and Joe allowed as how they'd win them back next Sunday at church, so I felt pretty good about it all.

I didn't forget my main mission in the heat of the game, neither. I knew the Porters' pa did farrier work and sometimes went around to those who didn't have the time to come into his shop in town.

"Say, Joe," I said, casual-like. "Your pa been doing much traveling out of town lately for shoeing horses?"

He was concentrating, knuckling down on his next shot. "Same as usual. Every couple of weeks he slings his gear in a wagon and takes off for them's too busy to get into New Hope." He shut one eye and made his move, a nice clean hit, right out of the ring. "Got Jim's blue mib back from you, Jack!" He looked up, grinning. "Swopes need some work done? I'll pass it on to my pa."

"Nah, but I figured the Petersons might. They hardly ever get into town anymore."

"Pa already took care of them last week," threw in Jim. "Strange sort of place it is, too, the times I tagged along. They got a slew of youngsters, but never once seen any of 'em around, begging for the cast-off shoes to play with, like others we go to."

"Didn't say nothing about Mandy from this visit, did he?"

"Nope. Hardly ever see Mrs. Peterson, either. The mister keeps us down to the barn the whole time."

"That's not too far from the Swopes', is it?"

"Thinking on visiting Mandy?" asked Joe, like he was interested.

"I might, just."

"You figure that ink I poured on her hair last week of school is finally wore off? It hung on pretty well into June." He grinned. "She took it awful good, much better than that prissy Sue Ellen would of."

"And if Mrs. Bergman wouldn't of died, Mandy'd have shown you a few things this summer, on account of that ink, Joe Porter."

"You know I didn't mean nothing by it, Jack. It was

just one of them irresistible temptations the Reverend's always going on about."

Well, then, I finally got it out of him. It was complicated, but I memorized the directions Joe give me, with Jim throwing in additions:

Follow the road on the west side of the Swopes' corn field right on into Lahaska, then take the road to Pineville, but don't stay on it more than a mile. When you come to a stone house with no roof, go right on the track, then past a frame house and a melon field to a guidepost. There you take the road south with sheep grazing on either side, follow a faint trail past some haystacks, cross a crick, and on the other side ought to be the Petersons'.

Those directions should of been clear as day. Unfortunately, right now it weren't day. Out there in the middle of the night, riding bareback for the first long piece on Pie, they seemed dim as the starless sky to me, specially since I'd never been anywhere in Pennsylvania except between New Hope and the Swopes' outbuildings. But it was an adventure. I could tell Pie thought so, same as me. He kept his head up, just snuffling the good night smells, trotting along at a lively pace, acting sheer happy to be alive. The first heat flash and sound of thunder shook him a little, then he ignored the rest.

We must have gone a couple of miles at least. I'd been able to get through the sleeping town of Lahaska and onto the Pineville Road, but hadn't yet found the roofless stone house. I went on a ways more and it suddenly loomed up at me. Abandoned. Even at night, it didn't look like anybody'd lived around it for some time. It made me think that maybe somebody else was wandering around in the night looking for a home. The melon field was something else. I could see fat, round shapes sticking up as we passed, at a walk now. How'd they get them to grow so big? Wouldn't one of them taste good cut open right about now. The Swopes didn't believe in such delicacies. If you couldn't store or can it for the winter, it weren't worth growing, to their minds.

My mouth was still watering after them melons when I passed the guidepost and went down into the sheep country. Now that I'd got this far, I wasn't sure what I was supposed to do next. I'd come to see Mandy, but how was I going to find her? Especially without waking all the Petersons? I had a feeling that wouldn't be a good idea, somehow.

Then we were at the crick. Just past it, I could see a rectangular shape outlined against the night sky. It was an unusual shape for farming country and it didn't seem to fit in with the softness of the hills around.

I slid off Pie's back and let him drink from the crick till he'd had enough, while I considered the lay of the land. I patted him and thanked him for the good ride, then took the precaution to hobble him with a bit of rawhide I'd stuffed in my pocket for the purpose. Just by the way his nostrils were moving off toward the mountains, I knew he was smelling something close to freedom. I'd of liked to set him loose someday, but that wasn't the sort of thing you could do in Pennsylvania. It'd been civilized for too long. Every piece of dirt, rich or rocky, seemed to belong to somebody.

I pulled off my boots and walked across the few yards of crick to the other side. The water felt cool and good. I still wasn't sure what my next move would be, but some lightning lit up the sky then and gave me a better look at the Peterson spread. There was a barn, like the Swopes had, and a little, low-walled pen built of stone next to it. There were a few dirty-white lumps laying down in there. Must be sheep. The sky lit up again. The house was smaller than I'd thought. Not only didn't it have a second floor, but it wasn't hardly a house. It was more like a ramshackle collection of leftover lumber and tar paper and flattened tin cans and such like that had been thrown together willy-nilly. It beat me how nine or ten of them Petersons could all find laying-down space inside of it. I slipped my boots back on and walked closer.

They weren't all inside. There was a pile of bodies curled up under the roof of the porch that'd been jury-rigged onto the mess right above the front door. I snuck closer, hoping one of them was Mandy. Then my boot struck a stone and I stood stock-still. One of the bodies moved. A head came up. I wasn't more than ten yards away. I stooped down, waiting. I saw the head move around, then the body ease itself up, wearily. It was a girl-child, all right, sleeping in her dress. She stepped over a few bodies and came out into the open. It was dark, but I could tell it was Mandy. Without a doubt. I stood up.

She looked like she was seeing a ghost, then slowly came out to me, like a sleepwalker. "Jack." It was a whispered prayer. "No, it couldn't ever be."

"It is." I took her hand, to show I was real, then pulled

her away. We didn't talk till we got down to the crick, with Pie waiting for me, all patience, on the other side.

Then she said it again. "Jack!"

The sky flared up again then and gave me a good look at her. What I saw made my heart most sink to my boots. Her hair was all sticking out and frayed. Her dress was filthy and torn. But that wasn't the worst. She was thinner than when I'd first met her, and her face was splotched, bruise-splotched all over.

"What have they done to you, girl?"

"Oh, Jack! They're worse than my pa ever was. And I swore I'd never take a beating from anybody, ever again!"

Then she was leaning up against me, sobbing, but no tears coming, as if they'd already run dry. I sank down on the ground, holding her. What was I supposed to do? Here all this time I'd been worked hard, with never a minute of rest. I'd been angered, too, by the tough, sullen Swopes. Maybe angered more by what they hadn't got, and couldn't give. Caring things I'd got used to at Mrs. Bergman's. Still, they'd fed me and hadn't really abused me none. They'd just treated me like an unpaid servant. All this time, I'd kept eating, and growing stronger with the work. All this time, what'd the Petersons been doing to Mandy?

"Talk to me, Mandy. I came as soon as ever I could. But if I'd known, if I'd known, it would've been much sooner."

"I believe you, Jack. I just knew you'd come. These people—they're not people!" She was angry now. "Closer to animals! They even took our dream book, Jack. They tore it up and used it for tinder!" And she started in with those dry sobs again.

"Hush. We'll get us another. It was only a book." What else could I say? We both knew it meant more than that.

"They took everything. Mrs. Peterson, she took my quilt. My Sunday dress from Mrs. Bergman, too. She gave it to her Gertie. I've got nothing but what's on my body."

"We'll make our own quilt, girl." She hardly heard my words, but I said them anyway, to try and calm her.

"And every day, every morning, just for the fun of it, Mr. Peterson, he lines up all the children, by size, and whips every one of us, right down the line. He whips me harder than the rest. To get me used to it, he says. It's the same thing before we go to bed. For everything we done wrong all day. When he's finished with us, he starts in on Mrs. Peterson. That's just the regular whippings. He sees you standing still one minute during the day, he stops everything and comes to cuff you again. He's much worse than my pa ever thought of being, Jack! My pa, he was just drunk mean. Mr. Peterson never touches a drop. He enjoys the meanness! There's not one inch of me isn't black and blue permanent, Jack!"

I listened to her. And the more I listened, the more I knew I couldn't leave her there. Not for one more night or day. I got up and fished out my handkerchief, then went down to the crick to wet it. When I came back, she was still lying there, no heart left in her.

"Come on, Mandy. Let me see your face. I know you got more spirit in you than this!"

She looked up and I swabbed her down some. Then I half lifted, half helped her up. She was too light.

"Where's your boots?"

"They took them, too."

"All right, then, we'll do without. Let's get going."

"You're taking me away?"

"You mean to stand there and think I'd leave you? After what you just said? They ruined your brain, too? Let's move, girl. It's a long way back. And we need to get there before daybreak."

I led Mandy across the water and right up to Pie.

"This here is Carrot Pie, Pie for short. He's my best friend now, next to you."

I let him sniff and nuzzle her a little so's he'd know she was my kin and all right. Then I hoisted her up.

"Hang on to the reins as well as you can. I've got to unhobble Pie and get up behind you."

Then we were on our way back, Mandy just leaning into me. I had a lot to think about, so we made most of the trip without hardly a word passing between us.

The storm that had been practicing up for nights now broke just past the roofless stone house. There was a crash of thunder like the sky had been rent in two. Hail—hail the size of small rocks—began to fall around us, on us. Pie was frightened out of his mind and took off in a gallop. I couldn't control him. I couldn't even look for shelter. I could only hold on to his slick sides with my boots, to his mane, with all the strength I had. I had to keep Mandy and me from being thrown.

Ever so slowly the hail slowed down and was replaced with a cold, hard rain. Pie was still spooked. I kept holding on for dear life and thanked the Lord when I saw the outline of the Swopes place. Pie ran right up to the paddock, like it offered some kind of shelter for him. I slid off, grabbed Mandy down, then led him through the gate. He didn't wait for me to rub him down. It wouldn't of helped much, anyway, in such a storm. I took Mandy to the house. There was a light on in the kitchen. Even the Swopes couldn't snore through a storm like this.

They was all up, watching the storm through the open door. Mrs. Swopes had put coffee on to boil. I pulled Mandy out of the rain and we stood there dripping, waiting for somebody to say something. They didn't seem to know what to say, just stood there in their nightshirts, Clifford and Amos with their mouths gaping open.

So I took the bull by the horns and looked right into Mr. Swopes's eyes. "I brought you a stray lamb, sir." Maybe the Bible part would soften him some. "This here is Mandy, and she—" But I didn't get no further than that, on account of Mandy just slid through my fingers and dropped in a heap on the floor. That woke them up.

Mrs. Swopes ran over in her robe and bent down. "What happened to this child? She's all over beat up."

I tried to get out about my night ride and the Petersons and all, but I guess I was done in, too, because next thing I felt myself sliding right down next to Mandy. And then I didn't remember nothing for a while.

I woke up in the good parlor. The one nobody ever went into. There wasn't much light coming in, because them heavy drapes of Mrs. Swopes was still drawn tight. It seemed to be some part of the daytime, though. I felt hot and squeamish, but roused myself, nevertheless. I was lying on a mattress on the floor, bundled up in some of Mrs. Swopes's best linen sheets. Mandy was next to me, wrapped likewise, but still asleep.

I got up, dizzy, and staggered over to the door and across the hall into the kitchen. Mrs. Swopes was cooking, as usual. She looked up from the heat of the stove. "You still poorly, boy?"

I flopped into one of them hardbacked chairs by the table. Then I nodded, just to be polite.

Mrs. Swopes came over and looked at me closer, then felt my head. "You got a fever. Best get back to bed, after I give you some soup."

"But my work—"

"The chores got done before you got here. Clifford and Amos can just roust themselves away from their tomfoolery with their horses for a while."

I could hardly believe how nice she was being. She didn't hug me or nothing like Mrs. Bergman would of, but Mrs. Swopes was doing her best as she saw it.

"Thank you, ma'am . . ."

"Hush up now and drink your soup. After it's done, you tell me something more about your Mandy. I stripped her down after the storm and cleaned her up. Whoever done that to her was worse than a sinner. It must have been the devil himself."

I choked on the broth. "She can stay, then? When she's fit, you'll just see what a help she can be for you. Why, she did most of Mrs. Bergman's laundry, and ironing and everything. And she knows how to sew right proper. And she'd be company for you, too—"

"Ssh. Don't go getting your hopes high, boy. Mr. Swopes don't know rightly what to make of all this. And Clifford and Amos, why, they're next to spitting mad you tricking them that way with the horses." Her eyes actually showed a little life. Pushed the dead look near out of 'em. "Clever little critter you must be at that. They still can't go nowheres near that stallion, and they been trying for two days now."

I spluttered again. "What two days?"

"You been out cold, boy. Or hot with the fever. You and your Mandy both. The only thing I can't figure is what did you do with that good wool blanket I give you?"

Well, I guessed it was pretty much all up now. So I told her about sleeping outside, and taming Pie nights. And about Mandy and her pa in New York, and the Petersons out here. She listened right up, the dead look changing more and more to flickers of interest, and sometimes anger. Then the soup was done and I sat there, waiting.

Mrs. Swopes, she was flexing those muscles in her arms now, like some kind of nervous tic. Finally she opened up. "I used to think I wanted me a girl. I had three of them, all in a row, all younger than the boys. They're buried out behind the church in New Hope. Still all in a row. They never made it past a few months. The middle one, she would of been like your Mandy now. About that old. It don't do to dwell on it none, though. The Lord didn't seem to be listening, and Mr. Swopes, he's got his boys, so he don't care, either."

She took the bowl away from me, absent-like, then

turned to look at me again. "Go on back to bed. We'll settle it all when you're both fit again."

I had that parlor memorized till I was feeling myself at last. In between these hot flushes that kept coming on, I noticed the drapes was a dark blue. And there were funny little fancy shelves screwed into two of the corners, wood scalloping all over the edges, and filled with crockery. I was lying down next to a kidney-shaped sofa, with big blue and red roses embroidered all over its seat and back. Then there was a clock and a picture over the fireplace mantel. The clock wasn't wound up, so I never did hear it tick or ring out. But the picture was pretty, what I could make out of it. It was one of them Currier and Ives things— I went up to read off of it when I was moving again. It had a big, shiny train engine in the middle, and rearing up on one side a powerful horse looking like it was trying to race that engine. The more I looked, the more I admired that picture.

Mandy slowly came around. She didn't say much at first. I guess she was just plumb wore out with everything. But she'd open her eyes, looking around real worried-like, and after spying me she'd smile and close them again for a while.

After another day I got up and went back to my chores, slowly, but nobody pushing me too hard for once. In between, I'd come in and take a look at her. Her shaking had stopped, and the fever was down. Her bruises were turning yellow from the black and blue they was.

Then, after another day, I saw her up in the kitchen when I come in for dinner. She was walking around, pretty as you please in her old dress, washed and mended, and one of Mrs. Swopes's aprons, tied up high under her arms. There she was, putting plates on the table, and getting down Mr. Swopes's Bible for the reading. I could of kissed her, but not in front of Mrs. Swopes.

"'Lo, Mandy, Mrs. Swopes."

"Jack! I was just telling Mrs. Swopes about that sticky flypaper in Mr. Richter's store. Don't you think it would be a blessing for her in this kitchen?"

I swatted away a few ornery examples. "Nothing but. That's for sure."

"She thinks maybe Mr. Swopes will buy some for her next time he goes in to New Hope, considering how he ain't going to lose his hay on account of that hail after all, and how the rain saved his corn. And—"

"Whoa. Slow down. You're all better now?"

"I'm wonderful, Jack! Mrs. Swopes says I can share the attic with you if Mr. Swopes don't object, and I've been up there. I think we can paint up the walls pretty, and make it as nice as our room at Mrs. Bergman's!"

I looked beyond Mandy to Mrs. Swopes. Seemed like she'd been doing more talking in my absence than I figured she was able. She was stirring something in a pot on the stove. Corn mush, probably, with maybe some bacon rinds thrown in. That was the usual for the noon meal. She looked different. Softer. Maybe she'd started in on forgiving the Lord and hoping again. Mandy had sure been busy.

Then Mr. Swopes and the boys come in and heaved themselves into their places. I took mine, too, at the end of the table. Mr. Swopes did the praying, and then the women started serving us. When we had everything they sat down, too.

Mr. Swopes didn't usually do much talking at the table, but I could see in his eyes that he was thinking on breaking his silence. I waited, just shooing the flies off my plate, not eating.

"You fixing on running off with that stallion again, Jack?"

"No, sir. Not on your life. It was only for Mandy, and I wouldn't of done that but I was worried after her." I stopped, afraid to say too much. But then he nodded like I should go on.

"And I done it with the horse, at night, so's I'd get there and back fast and not miss any of my chores. And I figure maybe you and the boys got yourself a good buy there. When he gets het up, Pie can run faster than anything I ever saw. I'll bet he could take one of them races at the fair, at that." It was about all there was to say, so I stopped.

Mr. Swopes, he ate a few bites. "That animal weren't ever meant to be trained for the flat races like that. Hope you ain't ruined him on pulling a sulky, or messed up his trotting gait." Then he thought some more. "But that ain't the principal problem. Peterson is. The man's got a bad temper. There'll be trouble over the girl."

I waited for Mrs. Swopes to say something on Mandy's account, but she didn't.

"He'll figure out sooner or later what come of her and be at our door."

"But you wouldn't let her go back, would you, sir? Not after what he done? You saw what he done!"

"The child's his property. We'll have to wait and see."

Mandy was hunkered down in her chair now, looking worried. She didn't look like anybody's property to me. I thought that was what the Civil War was fought over, Abraham Lincoln deciding that people couldn't be owned. Leastways, that's how Mr. Struthers had explained it. But somehow this didn't seem the moment to be bringing all that up.

"You're not going to tell Mr. Peterson we've got Mandy here, are you?"

"Can't spare the time to send somebody over right now. We'll be starting in with the mowing today, then there's the horse corn to bring in."

I breathed a sigh of relief. That gave us till after the harvest, at least. Maybe I could think of something by then. I dug into my mush. I'd need all the strength I could get.

But I'd forgotten that Mr. Peterson ran sheep, and not corn or cows. He didn't have no harvest to worry about. Three days later he rides onto the Swopes' farm, a deer rifle hanging by his side. Mr. Swopes and the boys were just coming back from the fields for the noon meal, red and sweaty all over from the work. I'd been out, too, but came back earlier to see after the livestock. Mandy was off to the side of the house, hanging up wash on the ropes tied there. She came around to see who it was, barreling in like that, then ran for the kitchen like somebody was out to kill her, which Peterson probably was.

I just froze to my spot and watched. Peterson got off his frothed-up horse and swung the rifle easy between his arm and body. He hadn't missed the sight of Mandy running like a scared chicken.

"Swopes. Looks like you got something that belongs to me."

Mr. Swopes was standing a few yards from Peterson now, sizing him up. They were about a size, Mr. Swopes beefy to Peterson's hardness. Clifford and Amos were off to the rear. They didn't give a fig one way or t'other about Mandy, but they'd like a good scrap, for sure.

"If you're referring to my stray lamb in there, Peterson, you got some explaining to do. The Lord says, 'Woe to the shepherds who are destroying the sheep of my pasture!' You ain't been such a good shepherd, seems like."

"Cows is your business. You don't know nothing about sheep, Swopes."

"I know you been leading yours astray."

"How I run my sheep and my family is nobody's business but mine."

His rifle was edging up now. It looked like a bad situation, all the way around. I didn't know what was coming next, and I sure didn't expect what did.

"Put that rifle down, Rolf Peterson!"

It was Mrs. Swopes at the kitchen door. And she had her mister's squirrel gun up to her shoulder, the one the boys had just had out to grease, getting excited about the hunting season coming up soon in the mountains. It was cocked and aimed straight as an arrow at Peterson's heart. It wasn't about to falter, neither. I knew that woman had steel in her when she made up her mind on something.

"Tell me what you want this child for! You got eight or nine others, last I counted."

"Still do. But a couple of 'em is down with busted limbs, and them the oldest, too. Need this girl to help out the wife like I took her in for to begin with."

"You're not going to break this one like you did the others, Rolf Peterson!"

"You don't know what you're talking about, woman. Brittle bones just seem to run in the family. A little discipline never hurt nobody."

"Get off our farm! If my husband don't have the guts to stand up to you, I will!"

Well, instead of putting his rifle down, Peterson lifted it real fast and let off a shot in Mrs. Swopes's direction. I thought he missed, but I didn't find out for certain till after it was all over. That bang finally woke up Mr. Swopes and he took a flying leap at Peterson, knocking his gun down. Even Mr. Swopes wouldn't stand on ceremony with his wife being shot at. Then Clifford and Amos jumped into the fray. Next thing I knew, everybody was kicking and pummeling each other something fierce, only Mr. Peterson caught aholt of his rifle again with one hand and started swinging it like a club.

At first I couldn't believe my eyes. This sort of thing happened out West, not in civilized Pennsylvania. Then I began edging in for my own licks. Almost made it, too. Only suddenly Peterson came out on top, with the Swopes laying back, dazed and winded. It was clear he'd whupped all three of them single-handed. He didn't even need to point that rifle again, just kept it at the ready.

"I don't expect any more neighborly discussions about my property. Send the girl out. Now."

I finally looked at Mrs. Swopes. It seemed like her

kneading arm had been singed by the shot, and the squirrel gun'd been dropped to the floor behind her. She turned around hard and sent Mandy out, never saying nothing else to the girl.

Well, I guess Mandy knew it was all over now. She walked out slow and steady and didn't fight when Peterson shifted her up onto the horse. Then he slung himself and his rifle behind her, gave the horse a vicious kick in the ribs, and they was gone.

Chapter 10

I T   W A S   S H E E R desperation that led me to my
next move. I lay out under the stars that night, finger-
ing the iron key still around my neck. The Swopes was
all tucked into bed nursing their wounds, not saying another word to me or each other about what happened.

I needed to talk to somebody about Mandy, and fast.
I thought it all over hard. I knew I'd promised not to take
Pie out again, but sometimes people are more important
than promises. I finally got up and whistled low for Pie
by the paddock. I opened the gate and mounted him fast,
before I could change my mind.

It didn't take long to ride those few miles into New
Hope. I galloped right down sleeping South Main Street
and up to Mrs. Bergman's old boardinghouse. It had sold
faster than anybody expected. That's probably 'cause no
one had expected those two old maiden ladies to make
an offer for it. So they was running it now, and I figured
Mr. Struthers had to be back from his trip. School couldn't
start without him, and I'd heard it'd opened up again last
week.

I knew which room was his, too. The corner front one

155

next to the parlor, facing the street and river. I tied Pie up at the fence, then went right through the border of flowers and banged on his window. Had to bang three times afore I heard his cough starting up.

Then he was looming up to his window, all stark and skinny edges in his white nightshirt. "What in the world—"

"It's me, Jack McConnell, sir."

He opened his window then. He was probably afeerd of the night air on his asthma. "I keep regular hours at the schoolhouse, young man. And you and Mandy have been absent since opening week."

"It's about Mandy I've come. Please. I've got to talk to you!"

"Just a minute, I'll let you in the front."

By the time he got there with a light, he'd pulled on trousers and was hacking into his huge handkerchief. Summering by the sea hadn't done him much good that I could tell. Then we were sitting in the parlor, me relating everything. He had to calm me down a few times so's I wouldn't wake the old ladies. Finally I was done. He fiddled with his handkerchief some more.

"You can help, can't you, sir?"

"I appreciate your trust in me, Jack. I genuinely do. Unfortunately, it's probably misplaced. I, personally, haven't the strength to go after your Mandy." He coughed again. "You see, during the summer I saw some specialists and they diagnosed tuberculosis—"

I jumped up indignantly. I could see he wasn't in any racing form, but it was his brains I'd come after. The Swopes' brawn hadn't worked worth a good spit.

"But you can talk to somebody. Somebody in town!"

"It seems to me the Petersons live in the next township. New Hope's authorities would have no jurisdiction over them. Besides, it would be hard, very hard to bring a case against a family who had willingly taken in an orphan—"

"What you're saying is orphans got no rights. None whatsoever! We don't count as people!"

"Now, Jack—"

I was already heading for the door. "Thank you for your time, Mr. Struthers. I'm sorry I woke you up, and I hope you feel better soon."

"Wait, Jack. Those sharks' teeth and fossils we talked about. I've saved some—"

I couldn't look back at him now, not with my eyes burning like they was.

"I'm glad you found some nice new rocks this summer. I hope their hardness gives you some consolation in your infirmity. Ain't no rock ever take the place of a real live person, though."

I knew that was a low shot soon as I got outside, but there wasn't any taking it back.

I hung on with the Swopes another two weeks, thinking things out, not that I had that much time for thinking. The harvesting went on from sunup till way past sunset. It was just as well. I didn't feel comfortable hanging around near the barn and house with Mrs. Swopes no more. Since Mandy'd been taken off, it was like a mask had come down over the woman's face. She went about all her chores just like before, only now there was even less interest in it all. It was like she was just doing her duty mechanical-like, as if she wound herself up like that clock in the parlor each morning, then ran down at night and fell into bed. At mealtimes she'd hardly look to the right or left of her, only bang the bowls down on the table and shovel in the food like she didn't know it was there at all.

And I'd worked my tail off for Mr. Swopes, but he acted like I wasn't around, either. Didn't talk to me unless it was a direct order for something that had to be done. Even the boys had stopped ordering me around and trying to find out how I'd tamed Pie, so they still couldn't get near him. It was like I wasn't there. Only I knew I was. Specially at the end of the day when my muscles ached all over.

It wasn't till nearly hog-butchering time that I struck up my nerve to ask about school. It was maybe a strange thing for me to be thinking about in the midst of all my troubles, but I had to think about something besides Mandy. At least until I worked out a solution. Not that I really wanted to see Mr. Struthers again, but it hadn't escaped me that, going to school, I'd get to see some of the town people on a regular basis, and maybe find somebody else who could help out with Mandy. It weren't that much of a straw, but a handful of straw was better than nothing.

I hadn't asked the Swopes thus far, and had worked like a dog on account of I figured they blamed their lost face with Peterson on me. It must be a hard thing for big people to lose a fight, especially three against one, like it was. Four, if you figured in Mrs. Swopes, too. And they must've been feeling it bad, because they hadn't even been to church service like I'd been counting on since the fight.

Well, it was mid-September now, and the harvesting about grinding to a halt. I couldn't see how they'd miss the boys or me too much, going off to school a few days. I knew I could ride Pie and be back in plenty of time before afternoon chores.

So, anyways, I finally got up my nerve and went to Mr. Swopes. He was out back, seeing to a sprained foreleg one of his Clydesdales seemed to have picked up. I stood around quiet-like and give him a hand with the liniment plaster he was fastening on. With a huge horse like a Clyde, it near took two people for the job.

Finally Swopes finished and looked on me like he hasn't seen me in weeks. "You're a good worker, boy, but I don't know that you've brought luck to this place. I should've maybe paid more attention to that verse out of Jeremiah when I plucked you down from the pulpit. 'For behold, I will send serpents, cockatrices, among you, which will not be charmed, and they shall bite you, saith the Lord.'" He gave me another look. "I can't truly say you're one of them serpents, but you brought others amongst me."

He said it, just like that, then moved on.

"I brought my wife to this farm fifteen years ago, and never had no enemies before. I could raise my head high when I went into town. Now I just think about making my enemies my footstool. Is that a Christian thought, boy?"

"'Revenge is mine,' says the Lord." I threw that in

so's he knew I was following his thinking. "Although sometimes it don't hurt to help the Lord along a little."

I'd been doing a lot of Bible reading lately, on account of there wasn't nothing else to read. A little reading before bed loosened me up some. There was only so many times you could reread Dickens and McGuffey's, and I'd just about memorized the Whittier. I looked back up at Mr. Swopes. It didn't seem the perfect moment to mention school. But would there come another?

"If I'm getting in your hair too much, you could send me off to school a few hours each day. Clifford and Amos, too, of course."

"Clifford and Amos done finished their formal education. They can read enough to work through the Bible. Ain't much more they'll be needing as farmers, is there."

He said that like a dead-certain fact. Wasn't no way I was going to convince him different.

"There're still a few things I wouldn't mind learning, though. I could save up a lot of the chores for evening, too. Course, I wouldn't expect to go past autumn and winter, with the spring planting to be done and all . . ."

"You read better than my boys. And I don't want no tales circulating about town."

"What kind of tales, sir?"

"You know what I'm referring to, boy. There'll be no more school for you."

He didn't leave me no room to argue. I guessed I was going to be stuck with the Swopes till I was big enough to make my own way out of here. How long would that be? Two or three years? More? I left Mr. Swopes leaning over the paddock rail and went off to think about that myself. It wasn't a heartening thought. And there wasn't any way in this world Mandy could stick it out that long at the Petersons', either.

When I came in for supper that evening, I was still considering it all. Mr. Swopes had made the milk run that morning while the boys and I had got on with the end of harvesting. Looked like he'd stopped in at Richter's General Store on the way back, 'cause there was some rolls of flypaper just sitting in the center of the table, unopened.

Well, I looked at that flypaper, and Mrs. Swopes looked at it, too. She must've been looking at it all day, from the way she set the table all around it. Neither of us said nothing, but before she served the food she hung it, right over the stove and the table, and that was the end of that.

That night I bridled up Pie and we set out for the Petersons' again.

The humps under the lean-to porch was fewer this time. And Mandy didn't seem to be among them, neither.

I had my boots strung around my neck and crept up real close to be certain-sure. No. They must be keeping her inside, after that last time. I stepped over the bodies and not a single one moved. Poor critters must be plumb used up. I poked my head in the door. More bodies all over the hard floor, without even a corn-shuck mat beneath them. I knew Mandy was in there. I could sense her.

She must've sensed me, too. She had a way of doing that. One of the heads came up, quiet-like. Then there was this grunt and an arm swang out from the only bed in the room and walloped her one.

"Told you not to be moving from that spot!"

"But I've got to use the privy!" It was whiny, not like Mandy's voice at all.

"Get on with you, then. You got two minutes afore I come after you with the strap."

"Yes, sir. I know, sir."

Then she was out, picking over the bodies, to the side of the house where I'd moved.

"Jack. Where are you, Jack?"

"Come over here, by the barn," I hissed.

She dragged herself over, and I noticed she was limping a little.

"What's the matter with your leg?"

"It's nothing."

I grabbed her, maybe too hard. "What is it!"

"Get your hands off me, Jack! I won't take meanness from you, too!"

"Mandy, Mandy! I'm sorry!"

Then she was hanging on to me again, breathing too hard. "I can't go with you again, Jack. Not this time. He said he'd kill you next, and Mrs. Swopes, too. I've got to stay."

I tried to hug her, but she wouldn't let me. She pulled away. "My time's up. I've got to go back or he'll come looking for me."

And that was all.

I hung around for a while trying to think of something to do. Nothing came to me. I got back on Pie and kicked him too hard, making him look back at me with a whinny of confusion.

"Sorry, boy. I shouldn't ought to have took it out on you. It ain't your fault."

We started back for the Swopes'. I think he forgave me.

I was all the way to the Swopes' and had Pie wiped down and back in his paddock before I could think clear again. I shouldn't of left Mandy there. I should've forced her to come with me. But it was too late for tonight. And deep down inside I knew that it wouldn't have worked. The girl wasn't budging. It was me she was trying to protect, and maybe even Mrs. Swopes, a little. I could try again to-morrow night, but Peterson was already suspicious. He might be on his guard, waiting for me. I had a strong respect for his hunting rifle—and his will to use it. He wouldn't think no more of shooting me and throwing me in the ground out back beyond his place than he would of bashing his own children. It was principle he was working on more than just wanting to hang on to another scrawny orphan. His will against the rest of the world. Ain't nothing was going to talk him out of Mandy now. And with me out of the way, life wouldn't be worth nothing to Mandy.

No, going back to the Petersons' wouldn't accomplish a blessed thing. So, tired as I was, I packed my belongings in my knapsack and went down to the paddock to say goodbye to Pie.

He was waiting for me, and I put my arm around his neck and buried my head in his mane. "I done the best I could for you, Pie, I just want you to know that. You try to be good, now. Let the boys near you. If they can't get you trained to racing, they're like to sell you off. I'll come back for you someday, when I've got money saved. I'll buy you fair and square, and maybe the two of us—" I stopped. "Maybe the three of us can head out West where you'd like to be. I'd take you now, but they'd set the police after me for sure, and that wouldn't be a help to anybody."

He was nuzzling at me, whinnying in my ear. I couldn't go on. I turned away and lit out for New York. There was only one more human I'd ever put my trust in, and it was to Miss Blackman I'd have to go next.

It took longer than I would've liked to get back to New York, not that I wasn't moving as fast as was possible. But I had to stop to work up a little bankroll for meals and ferry crossings. Mandy would've appreciated me taking her principles so to heart like that.

Anyhow, it was still the tail end of harvest time, and nearly every farm I come to was in need of a little extra help. Mostly I worked for my supper and a place to sleep, but once or twice I stayed a day to earn a few coins. I was out of practice in the bootblacking business, but my farming skills had been polished up just fine. I guess I had learned a few things since last winter, at that. And I had plenty of time to think on them while walking the long road, or maybe lying in the back of a hay wagon I'd hitched a ride with for a few miles.

First off—and this was so obvious it hardly even counted—first off, I missed not having Mandy trekking beside me. Once I got past that, though, there was other things to consider. I was more at ease out of the city now, less scared of going up to people and asking for a job, or a meal, or a bed. Country people as a whole weren't too bad, least not if you only asked a short-term favor like that. Specially if you was willing to work for it, and could do the work.

I got to putting these new people into categories, home-wise, knowing there was no chance anyhow. I right off the bat struck the elderly off my mental list of possibles. I wasn't going to settle me and Mandy down with another Mrs. Bergman who'd go and die off on us just when we was getting to really like her. Nope, my little list of possibles got headed off with: hale, hearty, and not too old. Not too old was a trick question, sometimes. What was too old? Thirty? Forty? Fifty? Shoot, I'd seen tenement women in New York used up at twenty.

Somehow, my mind always went back to Miss Black-man. I didn't even know how old she was—surely past twenty, but I didn't think quite thirty yet. At any rate, she always seemed about perfect. I'd be setting all these farmwives up against her. This one was already gone gray, that one was too harried, didn't have Miss Blackman's calm steadiness, the next one wouldn't never have the same kind look in her eyes.

I knew it weren't right of me, planning on throwing all my troubles in poor Miss Blackman's lap, and her only having seen me a few times, and Mandy never at all, but it kept me going.

As for the man of the family, it all come up in negatives, 'cause I couldn't fit any clear picture in my mind at all. I wouldn't mind giving up some of my responsibilities for a little security, long as I hung on to a feeling of freedom. But I sure didn't want a Peterson, Morressey, or Huffmaier, and I couldn't stomach a Swopes. Neither was I looking for a wishy-washy Mr. Struthers.

I worked the problem over and over, hoping deep inside there was some other kind of a man out there. It kept me busy in the time it took to get near to Jersey City and the ferryboat to New York. It wasn't a lot to go on, but I figured it was more than I had before.

It was late September already when I made it to the ferry. I rode across in daylight, remembering the last time, with me and Mandy and the flipped nickel. It was cold then, but now the breeze was refreshing, and the trees upriver on the Palisades had hardly started turning colors yet. Peterson's words, so casual they were, about his children with the busted limbs, kept repeating and repeating in my head till I thought I'd go crazy with them. Maybe I shouldn't have tarried those extra two days working the fields for money. But without the money I'd be trying to swim across this Hudson, or getting myself in trouble with another borrowed boat.

Of a sudden, the wind turned cold on my neck. I couldn't hardly wait for the ferry to dock, and was the first one off and racing uptown, my knapsack swaying on my back. I'd nearly made it all the way to Thirty-fifth and Broadway when a new thought occurred to me. A horrible one. What if Miss Blackman weren't at the Children's Aid Society? What if she'd gone off on another orphan train? Even worse, what if she'd married somebody and wasn't Miss Blackman anymore? I slowed from my dogged trot into a walk, the sweat pouring all over me. Why hadn't I thought on all this before leaving the Swopes'?

But it was too late. The brownstone house loomed up before me in the late-afternoon light. It looked different without the snow piled up around it. The stones were a softer, more pinkish tan. There was even a little box of geraniums out front. Red ones. I wondered who took the time to tend them. Then I stopped bolt upright near the door. A fresh horror hit me. Did I just march up and bang on the door? And risk facing Mr. Simmons? He'd collar me for sure and ship me off somewheres again. Lordy. What a fix!

I sat down then, right next to the geraniums, almost set to cry. I was that low I didn't pay no heed to all the passersby, nor the carts and such in the street, just hunkered down there in the veritable depths of despond. This was worse than any melodrama I ever took in on the Bowery. In my right mind, I would've at least took the occasion to dust off my blacking kit and make a few coins, but the heart wasn't even in me for that. And if I did find Miss Blackman, what would I say to her? Did I really figure all this time that she'd drop everything and run off on a rescue mission with an orphan she only seen a few times?

I was almost ready to start bashing my head into the nearest stone wall when a voice broke through my gloom. "No. It couldn't ever be. But, dear me, I think it is."

It was a soft voice. A sweet one. I looked up. "Miss Blackman?"

She was just like I remembered her: not too tall and not too short; gently round in all the right places; masses of thick blond hair piled up on her head, with little bangs fringing her forehead; all that topped by one of them big-brimmed flowerpot hats quality women liked. Hers had a rakish tilt to it that suited her. I just stared, memorizing every bit of her, I'd been that hungry to see her. She was dressed this time in a pretty green walking frock, all bits of lace around the collar and cuffs, and ruffles down her bosom. She must have been out shopping, for she carried a few parcels done up in brown paper and string, and a frilly parasol. My, but she was fine. Even her parcels took on a glow.

"Is it really my old friend Jack?"

Well, ain't nobody's heart ever took such a leap from low to high as mine did right then and there. "You remembered? You remembered me!"

Her parcels were down on the steps now and she was reaching out her arms for me. "And why not? Cook's had me worried silly, and praying for you, ever since she confessed that business in Jersey City last winter. And where's your cousin?"

That did it. I just threw myself into her arms and started in to bawl. I knew it weren't right, and it weren't grown up, and it were even silly, with help at hand like that. But I did it anyway.

Next thing you know, she was leading me into the house, right past Simmons's closed office door, right up the big steps past the dormitories, then up two final sets of stairs and into her very own room. There was a tea table fixed up and waiting for her, like we was expected. After helping me out of the knapsack, and pointing me to her washbasin, she sat me down in a delicate little chair opposite her and calmly began to pour us both a cup of tea.

I hiccoughed once or twice and started out trying to thank her for *Snow-Bound*, but she hushed me up. "Drink your tea first, young man, and have a slice of cake. Then you may tell me everything."

So that's what I did.

I was coming into the homestretch on Mandy's and my story, with Miss Blackman just listening and pouring more tea, her big blue eyes getting bigger and bigger all the time, when there was a knock on the door and Cook Murphy burst in. "Delivery boy just brought another one of them packages for you from that lovestruck cowboy out West, Miss Angeline. It ain't as heavy as the last one, though—"

Then she spotted me. "Jesus, Mary, and Joseph. It's a ghost I'm seein' for sure."

She blessed herself, fast, and stood there turning white, until Miss Blackman got up and gently pushed her back out the door.

"It's not a ghost at all, Cook. But Jack and I do need a little time in private to finish our talk. Thank you for the parcel. If it's another five pounds of jawbreakers, the children shall have them."

With Cook gone, Miss Blackman gave that parcel a bemused look and fixed to put it down.

"I'm just about finished up, ma'am. Don't let me keep you from your mail."

Well, she looked at the package again, then at me, then what did she do but blush! I hadn't been paying much attention to Cook's words, but I had caught the part about a cowboy out West.

"Got you an admirer, Miss Blackman?" I knew it weren't a polite question, but it might have some direct impact on my situation, specially if she was fixing to run after him anytime soon.

"Jack dear, it's a pity you missed that train. Nebraska was a revelation, particularly for an orphan like me who'd never been out of New York City."

"What! You an orphan, too, Miss Blackman? I never would of guessed—"

"Yes. Raised by the Society since I was younger than your Mandy."

I wanted to ask more, but her eyes were still on that package.

"Go ahead, open it. I couldn't wait if somebody sent me one. Only nobody ever did."

So she blushed again, ever so nicely, and laid into it. I couldn't figure the contents noway, though. It was licorice. Piles and piles of it. What kind of a cowboy courted a woman with jawbreakers and licorice?

She must of heard my mind, 'cause she started talking, then, like to herself, but aloud. "He sent me fancier things at first. Lovely beaded Indian moccasins, and once even a buffalo robe. But I sent them right back. They were inappropriate for a single woman to accept. You understand that, don't you?"

170

I didn't, but nodded anyway.

"Then he started in with the funny packages. Peppermint sticks and jawbreakers, and . . . and licorice!"

Her eyes met mine and she sighed. "Whatever am I expected to do?"

"What's he look like?"

She ignored the suspicion in my question and turned dreamy. "He's big. One of the biggest men I ever saw. And he's got all this curly red hair, and the thickest, reddest beard, and he's the stubbornest—" She stopped. "Now, why am I telling you about Red Rasmussen? We've got to be thinking about rescuing Mandy, and what to do with you. I wonder, if I spoke to Mr. Simmons—"

"Don't even think on that, ma'am. I won't be taking his charity, nor be beholden to him. It never worked out before." I brushed cake crumbs from my pants and stood up fast, almost tipping the frail chair over. "If I learned one thing, it's I've got to be my own master. I ain't asking nothing from you except a little thought on the subject of Mandy."

"Oh, dear." Her hands dropped the box of licorice onto the table. "You haven't had an easy time with grownups, have you."

"No, ma'am, but I'm getting older every day. Soon I'll be old enough to look 'em in the eye, man to man. I won't be needing them anymore, then. No offense to you, Miss Blackman."

She smiled. "Of course not. But where will you stay now?"

"I might try the Newspaperboys' Lodging House. Or find a roof of my own. But I'll keep in touch. I know you

171

can't think up something this very minute, and I'm not expecting it."

I was almost at the door when she stopped me. "Do you need anything else? Any money?"

"No, ma'am, and I wouldn't ever ask any from you, either, nor take it." I was standing as firm on my own two legs as I could now, as firm as I could while trying to work back into my knapsack, anyhow.

"Well, at least take some licorice!" And she stuffed a couple pounds into the back of my pack before I could protest, and a vast hunk of cake wrapped in a pretty embroidered napkin, too, I found out later. Then she gave me a big hug and I ran, before my big-shot words came back at me.

It turned out the Newspaperboys' Lodging House was already full up for the night, and I didn't feel like forking out money to stay in any tenement hall or flophouse. Not after spending all those summer nights under the stars. So I walked on over to the East River. Just as I'd remembered, the piers was still there. The water wasn't as fresh and clean by any means as the swift Delaware, but still it was running water. I'd got accustomed to the sound of the little stream gurgling on the Swopes place, and it was some comfort.

I hung around till it was good and dark and all the dockworkers gone home, then helped myself to a few cast-off wooden boxes. I lugged them under a pier just off the water's edge, where it was dark and safe, except for the rats. That's when I pulled out the licorice, thinking of making a supper from it, and discovered the cake Miss

Blackman had snuck in. I hadn't noticed before that it was a jelly roll. And Cook Murphy hadn't held back on the jelly part. I ate every crumb. Then I had a few sticks of licorice to top it off, spread out Mrs. Swopes's blanket, and popped right off to sleep. It was a relief having laid the whole worry on someone else's shoulders for a change. I didn't doubt for a minute that Miss Blackman would come up with something in time.

Chapter 11

MY FARMING MONEY didn't amount to much more than what it'd take for a hot meal a day for a week, so next morning I started right in on my old rounds, with the newspapers and bootblacking. I made sure and walked by Thirty-fifth and Broadway and the Society house at least twice a day, but didn't spot Miss Blackman. It was sheer painful to hold back like that, but grownups always did seem to work on a different time schedule than me. And if I hounded her too much, maybe she'd just give up on the whole thing. So I was giving her a few days' grace.

It was my third morning of making rounds past the Society that I discovered somebody else who seemed to be doing the same thing. It was a huge man, just kind of loitering around. He had on a wide-brimmed hat with a tall crown like I seen on some of the dime-novel covers set out West, and was standing like a rock in front of Miss Blackman's steps, turned away from me so's I couldn't see his face. I backed up a few yards and set up my bootblacking stand right there and then. I wasn't sure what I thought of his looks, and didn't want anyone bothering Miss Blackman should she feel like coming out for a stroll.

Well, the two of us played at ignoring each other for a while, me all the time sizing him up from the feet, which was my usual vantage point. He had big ones, with the funniest boots I ever saw on a man. They were pointy in the front, with a high heel in the back, and were scuffed up from travel, but you could still tell they was made of a fine leather. It was a kind I hadn't ever seen in all my business days, with little designs stitched into them over a kind of shiny black skin.

There I was, putting all my attention on them boots, when along trotted some of that old gang from Flynn's Bakery. I looked up long enough to note that the intervening months ain't done much for them. A rougher bunch I never saw. I watched them from my spot out of the corner of my eye, careful-like, since I didn't want no truck with them. They were up to something, sure and certain. And it weren't good.

It was Black Pete Finnigan, and Tim Hunter, and Buster and Tops, all right. I was considering making myself smaller, or fading into the sidewalk. There weren't either coppers or Mandy to get me out of a mess this time if they decided to take me on. I chanced another look, and blamed if they weren't ignoring me entire. All of 'em was still in a huddle a few houses down, eyeing this big guy I described in his funny boots and hat, and, come to think of it, funny clothes, too—just dark blue Levi's that fit like skin tucked into the boots, shirt sleeves under an open leather vest, and a red-and-white neckerchief I seen when he shifted sideways once. He sure wasn't dressed like a city man.

Before I could blink, the whole gang commenced fighting with each other, rough. And here they came, a-pummeling and rolling down the street toward this greenhorn. I pricked up fast. I been out of the city so long I almost missed what they was up to. They were about to barrel into him and rob him blind, or my name's not Jack McConnell.

It all happened faster than I expected. I opened my mouth. "Watch out, mister!"

But they were into him already. I bounced up and headed at an angle to cut off Black Pete Finnigan. He was always the point and pocket man.

Black Pete improved his technique some. Before that touch could hardly notice what'd happened, Pete was racing off, a fat wallet in hand. But I had a start on him, and I had a few pounds on him, too, after all those months of country food. It only took but one good fist in Black Pete's stomach and the wallet dropped into my hand. Then I raced back to the man while the gang scattered, yelling imprecations at me.

That greenhorn stood looking down at me from his great height, like he didn't know what had come off. Then he tipped back his hat, revealing curly red hair, while a big grin slowly broke out on his face. It was a nice face, even with all that red beard. Not exactly handsome, but strong and fresh. And his eyes looked straight at you, like you was somebody.

"Your wallet, mister. I got it back for you."

"You surely did at that, son. I don't know where my mind was." He stopped then and looked up at Miss Blackman's house. "Well, in truth I do, but that's neither here nor there. Nobody could of bushwhacked me like that back on my ranch, in my own territory."

Things was slowly beginning to click in my head. It took a while, but maybe I was finally growing some of those new brain cells Mr. Struthers had wished on me. This big man, this Redbeard, could he be—?

"What can I do to thank you?"

"Sir?" I had to pull myself back quick. No, it couldn't be. Had to be just one of them coincidences.

He was opening his wallet. "How about a reward?"

"No, sir, thank you all the same. You could let me shine up your boots, though. They look like they've traveled a piece."

He laughed then, a warm, booming laugh. "So they have, and so you may."

I ran for my kit and sat down right on the Society's steps, bold as you please, and started in with the work.

"I sure do admire these boots, sir. Never saw any quite like 'em before."

"Lizard skin." His eyes had refocused on the house again, over my head.

"And the heels? Never saw a city man with such heels, nor a farmer, neither."

"For riding the range. They keep your feet secure in the stirrups."

Well, he didn't seem to want to say anything more, so I kept my peace and got on with the job. And they did look good when I was done, too.

I gave it one more try as I flourished my rag around them a final time. "There you go, sir. Fine enough to court a lady in."

"What's that? How did you know—" Then he looked down at me again. "How much do I owe you?"

"Well, they're a bigger job than most boots, but seeing as how we're sort of neighbors here, I'll give you my bargain rates."

There was a hint of a twinkle in his eyes now. "And what would that be? You fixing on turning me into more of a sucker than I already been?"

"Never, sir. It's only a nickel I'm asking."

Well, then his eyes turned even brighter—a warm brown they was—and he fished into a trouser pocket. When his hand came up empty, he went for the wallet again. What he finally handed me was a five-dollar bill.

"I ain't got change, sir, but I can maybe run down the block to the nearest saloon for you."

"You're not old enough to be frequenting saloons, young man. And this is what I meant to be giving you all along. You've earned it for your honesty."

I couldn't stand it no more. "You've got to be him!"

"Who?"

"Red Rasmussen, Miss Blackman's beau."

"O-ho." He was grinning ear to ear now. "Stand you up right there, young sir, and tell me precisely how you know of the lady in question!"

Now that I'd let out the cat, there wasn't anything to do but tell it all, so I started in with a hit-and-run version and went wandering on, till he stopped me. "Whoa now! Slow down! There's even more here than meets the eye."

Then he pulled out a big gold watch on a chain from a shirt pocket and snapped it open. "Near enough noon to suit me. Let's find a good chow place and talk this over more reasonable, man to man."

And that was how I got to be friends with Miss Blackman's Redbeard.

"How'd you come to be a cowboy, Red?"

"Not cowboy, Jack, I hire men to do that. I own the whole shootin' match. Over three thousand steers and enough land to graze 'em on."

We were sitting over the remains of our pork chops, him with his elbows up on the tablecloth, comfortable-like. "Then you really could."

"Could what?"

"Afford to take care of Miss Blackman like she deserves."

He threw his head back and gave one of his great roars of laughter. I sure did admire his laugh. I knew I couldn't never grow to be as big as him, but if I ended up with a laugh like that, from deep down in the chest, I'd be satisfied.

"You're right there, Jack. I could afford to keep her, in style. I got everything you need to be happy out West: a comfortable ranch house built with my own hands; books to while away the long winter nights by the fire; horses and dogs and cats enough to suit anyone. I got me a river and water rights, and miles of prairie to admire. And I tell you it's a better view than all these city streets. A man hardly knows how to turn around here." He stopped in the midst of his list, the twinkle back again. "Got me

179

a few things they never heard of back here in the East, too."

My jaw had been dropping and my mouth almost watering over what he'd been saying. What else could he have that'd top all that? "Like what?"

"Got me prairie dogs, a whole village of 'em. Some of them even help out my cook in the kitchen."

I couldn't visualize that nohow. Besides, I hadn't the foggiest what a prairie dog was.

"Do they bark?"

"Not exactly, but they do talk to each other. They're a little like a cross between a chipmunk and a squirrel. Cutest critters you ever saw."

Then he whipped a piece of pencil stub from his vest pocket and started in to draw on the tablecloth. "They help turn the spit by the fire, like this—"

He drew up a little round cage thing, but I still couldn't hardly fathom it all. Think of having little wild creatures running in circles around your kitchen!

Well, this small talk went on for a piece, till he finally stopped and looked at me. "The fact is, Jack, I already have everything a man could possibly want—except a good wife."

"That's where Miss Blackman comes in," I added, completely unnecessarily.

He went on as if he hadn't heard me. "I knew it was right, the moment I laid eyes on her. I'd come into Lonesome—that's the nearest civilization to my ranch—for monthly supplies, and noticed there was some kind of social going on over at the church. I knew it had to be a social, since it wasn't even Sunday. So I mosey on over and poke my head in, and there were all these scrawny youngsters lined up at the front, and they were being auctioned off, seemed like. The ranchers and their missuses were up there poking and prodding and inspecting teeth. I never seen such a to-do outside a livestock sale."

So that's what'd happened to them orphan-train children, Zeb and all. It sounded a lot like me and Mandy at the New Hope Bible Baptist church. But Red was still going on, his eyes far away now, remembering.

"And suddenly there she was, this angel of light and goodness, just hovering behind them all . . ."

I was into his story as much as he now. "And what happened next?"

"Some big cow of a woman spies me—"

That'd be Miss Gertrude, all right.

"—and asks do I want to stand for one of the children. 'Hell, no,' I says. 'It's her I want!' " His eyes turned sad. "It must've been my use of profanity that put off Miss Blackman. I didn't mean to do it, but once in a while a man gets all het up."

"I know what you mean."

"You do?"

"I've got female problems, too."

"You don't say! Tell you what. Seeing as how you're my only friend so far in New York City, you help me with my Miss Blackman problem, then I'll help you with yours."

His words made me happy, but I didn't figure I could ever count on them, 'cause he had no idea of how deep my Mandy problem really was. But I did like him just fine and couldn't for the life of me understand why Miss

Blackman was making his life so miserable. Grownups did tend to complicate their affairs, though.

I set my mind back on Redbeard's problem. "But how can I help with you and Miss Blackman?"

"She talks to you. She won't talk to me! She won't even write a proper letter. Just little notes like 'Dear Mr. Rasmussen, Your new package arrived today. Thank you for your consideration. Sincerely, Miss Blackman.' Confound it, I don't even know her first name!"

"Angeline," I spit out, then wondered if I should have.

"Angeline?" His face lit up. "Why, son, that's perfect! There couldn't be a more perfect name for her! Angeline—"

Well, then he tested it a few dozen more times, just rolling it out on his tongue, till even I'd had enough. Here was this huge, rich, sensible, nice man acting the fool over a woman. Did love do that to a man? I sure and certain hoped it never did that to me!

"Mr. Rasmussen, sir. Red!"

"Yes?"

"Time's a-wasting. We got to have a plan. Tell me what you want me to do for you." I was thinking more clearly now, coming out from under the clouds of all this romance stuff. The sooner I did for him, the sooner I could ask a favor—a big one—in return.

"Why, nothing, Jack. Nothing more than just getting the woman to agree to sit down and talk to me."

"Is that all?"

"I believe I'm capable of taking it from there."

"You sure and certain?"

He looked at me and slapped some money down on the table. "I know what I want and I came East to get it. I can afford to hang around till she makes up her mind. But I do think it's time for action."

Dinner was over.

Chapter 12

THAT AFTERNOON I judged Miss Black-
man's period of grace to be officially terminated. I
told Red it wouldn't do him no good to hang around like
a sick mule on her front stoop like that, and sent him off
to see the sights—after we agreed to meet at his hotel
that evening. Then I marched up the steps and banged
on the door. I was on a mission now, like a messenger
boy, and wasn't about to let Simmons throw me out. As
it turned out, Cook Murphy answered the door. She
jumped again when she saw me, then sort of touched me
a little.

"It's Jack, all right, Cook, front and center, to see Miss
Blackman."

"And what about that other poor child—"

"It's about her I've come."

"Her? But—"

"I guess anybody with all the grandchildren you got
might have trouble keeping the girls separate from the
boys, Cook"—then I let up a little. "But truth to say,
Mandy was in disguise when you took us to Jersey City."

So she just threw up her hands and let me in. They got a miscellaneous crew of orphans wandering around the place again, looking sort of lost, like I remembered feeling. But I ignored them and finally tracked down Miss Blackman in the storeroom.

She set down some britches she was inspecting for wear when she spotted me. "Where have you been, Jack? You had me worried!"

"You need some help with that?" I dug into the bags she was hauling secondhand clothes out of and we worked together for a while.

"I've been wracking my brains, and I just haven't come up with a solution for Mandy yet."

"I know."

"You do?"

"It ain't an easy problem. But I figure I got a corner on it now, if you'll agree."

She put her fingers clear through the holes in the toe of an old sock, gave it a bewildered look, then pulled it off her hand. "How, Jack? What do I have to agree to?"

It was like I was the grownup now, and she the child. Her blond hair was coming down in little wisps on the side of her neck, and she looked warm from being inside the building all day. She'd even got the top two neck buttons of her shirtwaist undone for air.

"All you got to do is have a little talk with a friend of mine."

"And who might that be? Another orphan?"

I grinned. "Not hardly. But you'll like him fine once you get to know him better."

She pulled more donated clothing out of a bag. "Why all this mystery? You sound as if I ought to know this person already."

"Well, sort of." I stopped and took a big breath, then let it and the words out in a rush. "Fact of the matter is, Miss Blackman, you got a visitor from the West this morning. Don't know how you missed seeing him out front, but—" I wasn't sure I was going about this the right way. And she was looking at me like I was crazy. "Confound it all, Miss Blackman, what've you got against a fine man like Red Rasmussen?"

She dropped what was in her hands and leaned back against the shelves, like she needed them to hold her up. "Him? Here?"

"It's him all right, and he's here. And he said if you'd only consent to talk to him once, he'd help me save Mandy!"

Well, it didn't go exactly like that, but near enough.

"He did? Mr. Rasmussen said that?"

I could see this conversation weren't going anywhere fast. More in constant circles, like one of Red's prairie dogs in a spit cage.

"Miss Blackman, he's the uprightest man I've ever met. He's come clear East from Nebraska to see you, and it seems like an insult if you won't even say hello! What's he going to think of the manners of New York City folks?"

It took a while, but she finally pulled herself together enough to see a little bit of the light. Before I left, I had an appointment set up for the two to meet the next afternoon at a toney ice-cream parlor. I couldn't have 'em in a saloon, and a restaurant might not be proper enough for someone like Miss Blackman, unchaperoned and all. I left her still sorting through those clothes. I had a feeling the ragman was going to get the best of the litter in the morning.

Redbeard was staying at a class hotel. It had brass spittoons, and they was all shined. I poked my way through the jungle of potted palms to the desk and inquired as to his room number. The clerk just looked at me, sniffed, and turned away.

I banged on the counter to get his attention back. "Look here, you, I had a bath in the East River this morning, so's I know for a fact I don't smell that bad. Mr. Rasmussen is expecting me. I'm in his service."

Well, that was stretching things, too, but it done the trick. Soon I was sprinting up the carpeted steps to his third-floor room.

He opened the door after the first knock. "That you, Jack? Did you see Angeline? What did she say?"

I eased out of my knapsack slow. I'd been carrying it everywhere, since it wouldn't last five minutes under the docks where I been sleeping. Sure as certain some street arab worse off than me would make away with it.

Red couldn't stand the tension. "Out with it, boy!"

So I spit it out, and instead of dancing around like I expected, he just kind of sighed contentedly and picked up a big cigar to light.

Then he led me over to the desk by the window. "I knew you'd come through, Jack. Now it's just a matter of surviving the next twenty hours or so. I've been working hard at that already. Just see what I've been up to this afternoon. I've been inspecting some of your city's engineering feats. I thought I might pick up a few pointers for my windmills back home. You never mentioned that Brooklyn Bridge they're building, but I found it anyway, and bought myself a piece of it."

"You what?"

"Look here." He wafted a fancy certificate in front of my nose. "I'm a genuine stockholder now."

"Let me look at that!" I did, and groaned. "What you went and did was let yourself be taken by a confidence man. What'd he hit you up for?"

He was nonplussed. "Nonsense. I got it for a bargain. He came all the way down from a hundred bucks to a ten-dollar gold piece."

"Red." I gave him a look and sighed. "Red, you ain't going nowhere in this city anymore without me right beside you. Another few days and they'll clean you out, lock, stock, barrel, and ranch! Ain't you never read the *Police Gazette*? Don't you know these streets are filled with the biggest rogues in the world?"

Well, he didn't. But he still liked his ten-dollar Brooklyn Bridge certificate. It was printed up nice, I'd have to hand him that, with red-and-gold trim and everything. He just grinned and called it an "affordable object lesson," whatever that was, and said as how he'd frame it to hang on a wall back at his ranch.

Then he put that matter aside and looked at me. "Now it's your turn, Jack. I've got the whole evening free, and we've got to get through it somehow or other. I thought maybe we could take in some supper and a play. I've been hearing about a certain Miss Lillian Russell clear back in Nebraska. If I don't see her while I'm here, my ranch hands won't ever let me know the end of it."

Supper and a play! I groaned, louder than before. A year ago it would've been heaven, but a year ago I wasn't half crazy all the time worrying over Mandy.

"What's the matter, son? You got a sudden stitch somewhere?"

"No, sir. It's just that I've been as patient as I can be, but I ain't got an ounce of patience left anymore. Not even for Miss Lillian Russell. With the world practically coming to an end for Mandy and all—"

"Who's Mandy?"

"She's *my* female problem."

Red, he raised his eyebrows, then pointed to the couch by the wall. "Sit down, Jack. Maybe I've been underestimating your need. Tell me about this Mandy."

I did, and he listened respectfully all the way through. In fact, he took it as serious as I had his Miss Blackman problem. He was kind of pacing in front of me the whole time, then took out another cigar. "What you're telling me is God's truth, boy? It's none of these big-city confidence tricks?"

"I swear it. On my very life, which is all I've got, besides Mandy. And Miss Blackman, she'll verify it, all right."

"Then why the devil didn't you say something sooner?"

"Beg your pardon, sir, but I figured first I'd have to know you a little better, not having much luck in getting aid and assistance from grown men in the past. Also, I thought you might pay me more heed if I helped out with your problem."

He gave one of his great laughs, then turned more serious. "You're clever, at that. Always make sure of a man's fiber before you put your trust in him." Then he shoved out a vast paw. "Let's shake on it, man to man. As soon as I get Angeline settled, we'll go after your Mandy. It seems to me, since I'm already this far East, another few days sightseeing over to Pennsylvania won't hold back my ranch none."

So we had a night on the town, after all, with me not twitching too much with impatience. Maybe I'd learn to calm down about my worries like Red when I'd put on another ten or twenty years, but I wasn't sure about it at all. Not if my worries had anything to do with Mandy.

I ended up bunking on the couch in Red's rooms. I really didn't want to let him out of my sight now—not until events unfolded at the ice-cream parlor.

It come out better than I thought. Red was nervous as a cat the next afternoon. I'd polished up his boots again, for good luck, and we'd even gone and bought him a proper Eastern suit. He hated the paper collar and tie. Said it choked him so he couldn't think straight. But he done it nevertheless, muttering all the time that he guessed he ought to have a marrying suit anyhow. Myself, I thought that a mite anticipatory, but didn't say nothing.

We was in front of the ice-cream parlor a full hour early, and when Miss Blackman come along at last, it was a relief for both of us. She was a vision, sure. She must've been down at all them shops on the Lady's Mile, 'cause she come in what looked like a spanking-new dress, all pale blue eyelet and lace, just floating along with that white parasol of hers. She looked better than ice cream. Their eyes met, then it was like I wasn't there anymore. Red, he gave her his arm and they waltzed on through the door, leaving me in the cold. Least I thought so, but three minutes later, out comes Red long enough to hand me a huge bowl filled with about five scoops and bananas, and nuts, and sauce. When I looked up from taking inventory, he'd disappeared again.

Shoot, they could take all day now. I sat down on the sidewalk and dug in.

We walked Miss Blackman home, then back to Red's hotel in silence. Up in his room, he tore off his new clothes and got comfortable in his old ones again. Then he lit up one of his cigars, pulled out a bag, and started shoveling things into it from the wardrobe.

"You fixing on going somewhere?"

"What I'm fixing on, Jack, is a little trip to Pennsylvania. Seems to me I've a promise to keep."

"You mean—?"

"I mean I'm a man of my word, and Angeline a woman of hers. We'll take a train in the morning for Trenton, then hire a buggy to go across the river."

"We?"

"You and I and Angeline. Your little adopted sister Mandy will need a woman to look after her, when the rescuing's done, won't she?"

I near went wild with joy for about five minutes, then finally wound down. "But what about after? What about you and Miss Blackman?"

"It ain't as promising as I thought, but it ain't hopeless,

either. It seems she's got some nephew of her boss, what's his name?"

"Simmons."

"Simmons. Right. Simmons has got some nephew he's hot to marry her off to. Works in a bank or some-such." He looked at me. "Can you imagine my Angeline married to some runty, dull, and boring banker? She needs more of a challenge than that, does our girl. Why, I can just see her riding out over the prairies with me. I'd even buy her a sidesaddle if that's what she'd like, but between you and me, she'd look much better in britches astraddle her mount. I got one I already bought special for the purpose, a nice gentle little mare . . ." He sighed at the vision, then took notice of me again. "Of course, all that would be hard for you to understand, how it feels to be one with a really fine horse—"

"It ain't, neither!" I shook my head vehemently, and Red gave me a surprised look. "How's that, Jack?"

"I had me a horse, even trained him myself." Then I had to tell him about Pie. It felt good telling it all to somebody like him that would understand. I finally finished with the sad part, about leaving Pie with the Swopes.

"Why, Jack, you continue to amaze me, you truly do. A young man like you would appreciate my horse Ranger, too." He went off in transports over his Ranger for a while, till finally he got back to where we started. "Angeline. She'd be queen of the prairie. I just can't let her marry that dolt, obligation or no." Then he brightened up. "She did say as how she'd seriously consider my suit after I put my money where my mouth was, meaning your

Mandy's rescue. Not in those words, of course. But near enough to."

Well, I whooped some more, then started emptying drawers for him. I couldn't believe my turn in fortune. Please Lord, let it keep going like this for a while longer. And let Mandy hold up till we got to her.

The two of us was on our way to fetch Miss Blackman in a hackney the next morning when something occurred to me. "How's Miss Blackman gonna come traipsing around the country with us? I mean, she's an unmarried lady and all—"

"She assured me she could gain permission from Mr. Simmons."

"You ain't never met Simmons. I just don't see him—" But then we'd arrived at the Society house, and Red was jumping down, giving instructions to the driver to wait. There wasn't nothing but for me to follow, my mind uneasy now. Things had just been too smooth. Something had to go wrong.

Cook let us in, a worried expression on her face. I fixed my eyes on the stairs, expecting Miss Blackman to come down them. Instead, the door to Simmons's office burst open, and out he came, bristling, Miss Blackman three steps behind. "Sir! You, Rasmussen, or whatever your name might be. What right have you to carry off Miss Blackman on this wild-goose chase?"

"You speaking up for her? You her father or something?"

That stopped Simmons for a moment, but then I got to

hand it to him, he did stand up for Miss Blackman like a man.

"I am certainly not her father, no. But I am her legal guardian, or the closest approximation thereto. You may consider Miss Blackman under my protection, as she has been under the protection of the Society since her childhood."

Well, that stopped Red a moment. He looked at Miss Blackman, a little puzzled, then came back strong. "Is she an orphan, too? Maybe I ought to compliment you, then. I never knew you could raise 'em up so fine."

Simmons didn't know how to take that, so Redbeard, he just kept plugging away.

"It's you I've got to ask for her hand, then. Well, I'll do it, formal and official, just like you were her own pa, although I had planned on waiting till we got back from our little trip." He stopped then, as if to catch his breath for what was coming. He cast a glance at Miss Blackman still hovering behind, the rough edges going all sort of soft as he did it. Then he started in again, ignoring me pulling at his sleeve, trying to slow him down before he got into trouble. It didn't help.

"She won't be needing any dowry. My prospects are just fine. I've got a ranch spread, near fifty miles out from Lonesome—that's in Nebraska, where we first met. Acres and acres it is, going right over into the territories, with a branch of the White River coming through a fair piece, for which I got waterin' rights."

He went on to list his other amenities, adding a few things he didn't already pass on to me. Then he stopped and beamed at Simmons. There wasn't any question in his mind but he was fully astride the situation.

Simmons must of thought different, though, especially with that nephew of his tucked away in the wings. Red clear forgot to mention that nephew at all. Anyway, all the way through Redbeard's recitation, Simmons was growing redder and redder in the face, standing taller, too, almost filling out. Didn't hardly look like the same pale, wan, pinched man I'd first seen in that tenement hallway.

"Mr. Rasmussen! Sir! Albeit on the very outer fringes, your state of Nebraska is still part of the glorious Union. Which is considered a civilized nation amongst most men. It is inconceivable that you can act like some sort of a Vandal or Viking and just waltz in here and take a woman when you feel like it! Miss Blackman has been raised like a young lady of quality. She has prospects in this city. Under no circumstances could I give my permission to such a thing as you suggest."

Redbeard got all kind of tight at the mention of "prospects" and began to glare at Simmons. I didn't like the look of his fists, which were beginning to ball up of their own accord. He could of squashed all of Black Pete's gang easy, if his mind hadn't been on other things, and it would take less effort to do the same to Simmons. Which might have given me some satisfaction earlier on, but not now. Not when Simmons looked to be genuinely concerned over Miss Blackman.

"How come nobody asked Miss Blackman what she wants?"

Both men stopped cold and looked down in surprise at me. The thought of having Miss Blackman speak for herself hadn't ever occurred to either of them. They turned kind of slow to look at her, and Miss Blackman opened up.

"From the mouth of a child . . ." She gave me a little smile, then turned back to the two of them. "Mr. Simmons, I am over twenty-one and therefore able to think for myself. This journey I set out upon has not been lightly undertaken. It is, instead, to find and give succor to a child who has fallen into the wrong hands. You and the Society saved me from just such a dilemma a number of years ago. Have you and the Society changed so much in that time? I pray not. Such a mission should not be deleterious to my reputation in any manner. Not even your nephew could hold it against me, I hope?" She paused then to give Simmons the eye.

"Mr. Rasmussen gallantly, I thought, offered me support in this undertaking but yesterday afternoon. At that time he promised not to press his suit further until we found success, thereby giving me further time to consider my options." She turned to Red. "You disappoint me, sir. I had thought you more high-minded than this."

Poor Redbeard, he kind of wilted under her scorn. And me, I'm ready to scream. Just because he goes and gets carried away, Mandy and me are going to be out in the cold again, without help. It ain't right. It just ain't right to have Mandy still suffering on account of some grownups can't get their minds together to act.

"Well, that's it, then," I said to nobody in particular.

"I guess I gotta hike on back to New Hope and get Mandy any way I can work it."

And I turned to leave. I figured on getting my pack from the cab and heading for the Hudson again. That five-dollar bill I still got from Red should see me all the way to the Petersons' easy. And I could always stop by the Swopes' and steal Pie. Then I'd swoop down, irregardless of Peterson's gun, carry off Mandy, and gallop into the sunset, always West.

I turned back again. "But I want you to know it's leading me into a life of crime, you are. And all this time I been trying to make a go of it on the straight and narrow, like my ma would've wanted."

I was almost to the door before any one of them budged. Then it was Miss Blackman who spoke up. "Jack. Wait! I'm going along, with or without male accompaniment."

Well, what kind of a creature she thought I was, I weren't sure. All these years I'd been pretty confident I was a male of the species. But I slowed down to see what else might transpire.

Red finally moved. "You'll need protection, Angel— Miss Blackman. My offer of assistance is still good. Without any strings." He turned to Simmons. "I swear your ward will be treated as nothing but a lady. I will protect her and her honor with my very life." Then he turned around and stomped out, adding, "It sure as hell isn't worth anything without her anyhow."

Chapter 13

SO THAT'S HOW our rescue trip got off to a start. It weren't as promising as I'd hoped. The train ride passed, and we got the buggy rented, drove up the nine miles from Trenton to the bridge at Taylorsville, and started in across the river to New Hope. I just sat between Redbeard and Miss Blackman the whole blessed time, listening to their silence. Don't think they said two words to each other all day. Neither of them seemed to be in choice spirits.

Not that I didn't have plenty to think on, myself. Before this day had started, I'd been dreaming that when we picked up Mandy, why then Redbeard and Miss Blackman would just naturally decide to adopt us both. There we'd be, the two of us, happy as clams in the lap of luxury out West. But as the day wore on and the silence deepened, the thought took me that a fine house and plenty of food and land weren't everything. If Redbeard and Miss Blackman weren't going to get back to their original feelings for each other, that house wouldn't be a fit place to live in. No place at all. Mandy and me would be miserable.

Why grown people could get themselves into such dithers beat me, but I could see from Redbeard's face on one side of me that he was in a black state. Then there was Miss Blackman on the other side looking like she was wondering why she'd ever scorned Simmons's odious nephew and gotten herself mixed up with orphan troubles.

We drove all the way through New Hope and were halfway to the Swopes' when all of a sudden we noticed it was getting dark. It was the evening coming, yes, but it was rain coming, too.

"We should have stayed over for the night at that boardinghouse back there." It was the first we'd heard from Redbeard in what seemed like hours.

"Maybe we should turn back, Mr. Rasmussen?"

"Too late. I never turn back, Miss Blackman. Not once I set my mind to something."

"Night might be the best time for the rescue anyway," I throw in, trying smooth things down. "And the rain might cover us, too."

"I'm thinking the same as you, Jack. But we'll need us a base of operations. Out of the rain. Especially if you figure it's still another ten, twelve miles to the Petersons'."

I didn't want to suggest it, but there didn't seem no other choice. I said it real low, though, so maybe they wouldn't hear it. "There's always the Swopes."

"Would they take kindly to seeing you again, Jack, after you ran out on them?"

"I ain't sure, Red. Not sure at all." And I wasn't, either. My obligations to the Swopes had suddenly come front

199

and center to my mind. They'd fed me, after all. I should've maybe at least left a note of thanks and explanation when I left. Maybe obligations wasn't all one-sided and on the part of grownups.

"It looks like our only choice. Give me directions."

The rain was starting to come down heavy by the time we turned onto Swopes land. Miss Blackman's parasol was trying hard, but it weren't ever intended to do service in a good country storm. Water was streaming down Red's beard, too, but he didn't seem to even notice it. Me, I been out in worse, so I just jumped down from the buggy and gave a good look toward the paddock by the barn, hoping to gain a quick sight of Pie. That would be a strong consolation for having had to come back. I could see right off he ain't out, though, so I headed for the back door, all the time figuring on how was I going to apologize for disappearing on the Swopes like that.

The whole family must of heard us, 'cause they started showing up, Mr. Swopes and the boys from the barn, and Mrs. Swopes poking her head through the kitchen door.

"Jack?" It was Mrs. Swopes took notice of me first. "Jack? Is that you come back?"

"Yes, ma'am. Beggin' your pardon for any inconvenience I give you, leaving like I did—"

She was brushing past me now. "You come in a buggy, boy? With visitors?"

"Yes, ma'am—"

"A lady, even! Where's your manners? Invite them in out of the weather, Jack!"

All this sudden enthusiasm had me a little bewildered, but I managed to herd Red and Miss Blackman in all right, followed by the rest of the Swopes. Then we all stood around the kitchen dripping and staring at each other. Mrs. Swopes was staring at Miss Blackman the hardest. I thought she was maybe staring at the long, delicate fingers resting on my shoulder—fingers that hadn't seen a lot of lye soap; and the fine cloth of Miss Blackman's outfit, even if it was damp and travel-mussed. Finally, I figured somebody's got to do the introductions, so I started off.

"Mrs. Swopes? This here is Miss Blackman. Miss Angeline Blackman. Clear from New York City and the Children's Aid Society—" I had to stop when Mrs. Swopes gave a little bob of a curtsy. Mrs. Swopes giving a curtsy? I pulled together again and pointed to Red. "And this is Mr. Rasmussen, from Nebraska." I turned around. "That there is Mr. Swopes and Clifford and Amos." I stopped again, then looked at the Swopes and figured I'd better say something good about them. "They took me on when Mrs. Bergman died."

The wind came up and shoved a good blast of rain through the still-open kitchen door. Miss Blackman shivered and pulled her damp shawl tighter against her body. She finally spoke up. "Might we stay for a few moments to dry off and talk? I realize it is an awkward time to be calling, but perhaps—"

Well, in another moment Mrs. Swopes led Miss Blackman and Red right through that kitchen, across the hall, and into the parlor! My. Ain't nobody been in there since

Mandy and I been sick. I was looking at Mrs. Swopes, curious-like, and I saw she was all worked up now, straight out of her funk.

"Light the fire, Felix. Our visitors have had a long, wet ride."

"Sure thing, Essie. I might as well come in and set, too. Till we figure out what's doing. Clifford! See that the coffeepot's on the hob for your mama."

Felix? Essie? I'd clean forgot the Swopes owned real names. And Clifford checking the coffeepot? The whole time I stayed with them, Clifford never been closer to the stove than stealing a corn fritter. And he went and done it, too!

Mr. Swopes was still going on. "The Good Book tells us to be hospitable, Miss Blackman, Mr. Rasmussen. Just sit yourself there on the sofa, if you please. Amos, take the lady's wet shawl."

Well, all this hospitality took a while to settle down. But by and by we was all sitting there drinking coffee and eating slices from one of Mrs. Swopes's apple pies, and everybody acting like I never even run away. I decided I might as well enjoy my pie and worry about the Swopes's righteous wrath later.

Miss Blackman finished hers first, then put her plate down, all gentility, on the whatnot table next to the little sofa. She looked across to Mrs. Swopes in the rocking chair by the fire. "Your parlor is lovely, Mrs. Swopes. And this sofa! Did you do the needlework on all of these roses?"

Mrs. Swopes, her face lit right up. "I did. Back before the children start coming."

"You have an excellent hand. Far nicer than much work that I've seen in New York."

Well, I can tell now that Mrs. Swopes's whole year has just been made.

But Miss Blackman don't stop there. "And I wish I could make a pie like yours. But I never had the benefit of a mother's loving training. You see, Mrs. Swopes, Mr. Swopes"—she looked at both of them sweetly—"you see, I was an orphan myself."

"Well, I never!" Mrs. Swopes gasped like she couldn't ever believe that. "A fine lady like you?"

"It's quite true. I've been raised by the Children's Aid Society since my childhood. Perhaps that will help you to understand why I take . . . why I take an unusual interest in what I call 'my children.' Jack, here, for instance." And she patted my head where I was sitting on the rug in front of her, till I turned red clear through to my ears.

"Jack was one of my special boys. We lost track of each other last winter when I had to go out West, but Jack came all the way back to New York to find me again. Mr. Rasmussen"—she nodded at Red, who'd been standing stiffly by the picture on the mantel all this time, taking furtive glances at that horse racing the locomotive—"Mr. Rasmussen kindly agreed to accompany us on our journey. We've come with the Society's blessings—"

I kind of jumped at that, and Miss Blackman touched my back softly, as if to say it was all right to stretch the truth a little, once in a while, and for a good cause like Mandy.

"—with the Society's blessings to check on Jack's

adopted sister. Even though we didn't officially place her, we are interested in her welfare. It's something we do every so often. We want *everyone* to be satisfied with their new arrangements after they've left the city."

Miss Blackman, she paused then delicately, waiting for her point to be took. Didn't take too long. Mr. Swopes cleared his throat, then spoke up. "Young Jack was doin' fine, up until he ran off last month, just as you can see. He got himself into one or two scrapes, but I guess that's part of growing up, for a boy. My Clifford and Amos do the same. Still, he could of give us some notice." He stopped to look at me. "Took off just afore the hog butchering, and we was counting on his assistance. Now here he is, back, like the prodigal son." He sighed. "The Bible says to forgive, so I guess we'll have to. If he ain't planning on doing more of the same any time soon."

Mr. Swopes, he made it sound like I was fixing all the time to come right back and finish off my life with them. That weren't never my intention, so help me. Not even for Pie.

I gave Red a scared look and he interpreted my panic rightly. "Jack's disposition isn't the problem right now. We'll worry about him after we've taken care of his Mandy."

Miss Blackman took over smoothly from there. "And have you heard something from Mandy? She and Jack are like blood kin, you know. Probably closer."

By now I got nothing but more admiration for Miss Blackman. How she could get to the point so nice without letting on she knows what's really happening, without offending no one, is sheer marvelous. I looked around.

Clifford and Amos, they're lodged up against the wall by the door, nudging each other over the Mandy business. Mrs. Swopes looks pained, and Mr. Swopes clear uncomfortable.

It was Mr. Swopes who had to say something sooner or later, and he finally did. "We had the girl visiting a spell back. She was fine when she left."

Mr. Swopes must've been taking lessons from Miss Blackman. Never knew a person could say the clean truth and be lying through his teeth the whole time like that.

Miss Blackman smiled brightly. "Well, that's wonderful. Any idea how she might be now?"

He shrugged. "I ain't my brother's keeper."

Miss Blackman, she glossed right over that remark like she hadn't heard it at all. "Jack mentioned that the Petersons' place wasn't that much farther down the road from you. Is that what you'd call it out here, 'down the road'?" She looked around for a nod from someone, anyone. They sat or stood like lumps. "Well, anyway, Mr. Rasmussen and I have rented the buggy for a few days. And if you'd be kind enough to favor us with directions, we intend to pay Mandy a visit as well."

Swopes shrugged again. "No harm in giving directions. The Petersons, though, well . . . They're a mite peculiar in their ways. No telling how they'd take to a visitor. Any visitor. Especially a fine lady and gentleman like you two."

Red broke in then. "We thank you for the thought, but intend to try." He pushed away from the wall. "I guess Jack can direct us well enough, anyhow."

Mr. Swopes, he gave a start. "You planning on running

off with our boy again? Seeing as how he's back, I figured on putting him on the milk route in the morning. It'd free up Amos and Clifford for some fall plowing."

Red smiled a tight smile. "I said as how we'd work out the boy's disposition later, Swopes. I'm thinking we'll need him to identify the girl once we get out to the Petersons'."

"Since you put it that way," said Mr. Swopes, "I guess we can manage for a day or two."

Before anything else could happen, Miss Blackman got up, smoothing down her skirts. "That settles it, then. Mrs. Swopes? Your hospitality has been delightful! I wonder if I could stretch it just a bit farther and ask for maybe a little picnic basket for when we find Mandy? Mr. Rasmussen?"

Red looked at her.

"Mr. Rasmussen, you mentioned that the horses were tiring. Perhaps Mr. Swopes would be willing to rent us replacements?"

It was Clifford who opened his mouth next. "Nothin' but a fool would go out there now, in the night and rain!"

"It's what we came for, young man," answered Red, decisive-like. "Never put off till tomorrow what could be accomplished today."

We rented the two Clydesdales from Mr. Swopes and Red gave me permission to drive, since I knew the horses and the way. I was sitting up in the buggy, holding the harness in my hands, feeling mighty grown up with Miss Blackman and Red sitting next to me, relying on me. Our things were tossed in behind us, next to the food basket Mrs.

Swopes had prepared. I looked over to the empty paddock once to say goodbye again in my mind to Pie.

He'd been in his stall in the barn when we'd gone after the team, and he like to went crazy when he caught wind of me. He kicked up something fierce till I ran over to hug him.

Red, he followed me. "This your horse, Jack?"

Well, I guess he could of known from the light in my eyes. They sure felt like they was shining brighter than the lantern.

"Yes, sir. This is Pie."

Red, he took Pie's head in his great hands and looked him over good, and Pie never even protested.

Then Red looked at me. "You've got good taste in horseflesh, Jack. I wouldn't mind this one as a breeder on my ranch. I like spirit in man and beast."

Swopes must of heard some of that as he was hauling out the team, 'cause he steps over lively. "Wouldn't recommend that one, Rasmussen. Me and the boys ain't been able to do a thing with him. And we had hopes on training him for the harness races. Fact is, we're giving up on him. I got a trader coming by in a few days to take him off our hands. There's no point in feeding him all winter if he ain't gonna perform."

Red just nodded like he was agreeing, then left me to finish off my new set of goodbyes. Now they was even harder. If Swopes sold off Pie, I'd never find him again. I nearly set to crying right then and there, before remembering my main mission. Mandy.

Life hadn't ever been this complicated before I took up with that girl last winter. There'd just been me to feed

207

and fuss about. Just one body to keep alive, and no non-stop worry. Without Mandy, I'd probably still be set up at Fred Huffmaier's, stoking his oven. It would've been a whole sight easier.

Then I pictured Mandy again, like I seen her last, all black and blue and practically lame. A hot feeling came all over me. I rubbed my head against Pie's a final time. If I hadn't met up with Mandy, I never would have found Pie, or Miss Blackman, or Red. I would've just been alone in my little cellar cubbyhole, just me and the oven and the *Police Gazette*s. I'd do it all over again in a flash. Being alone, even without worries, couldn't hold a candle to belonging to somebody. And the somebody I belonged to needed me now. I broke away from Pie and went out into the rain.

As I nudged the horses along with the buggy whip, I tried to make some small talk, thinking maybe to get rid of the queasiness I got in my stomach. All the things that could go wrong with Mandy's rescue seemed to have settled down there like hard rocks on top of my apple-pie supper.

Didn't know what to say to Red, since he hadn't done much at the Swopes' save look strong and determined. I guessed social graces weren't his cup of tea, and probably neither was Pennsylvania. So I turned to Miss Blackman first. "You were sheer wonderful, Miss Blackman, ma'am. I never seen anything like how you worked them Swopes. How'd you learn to do like that with you hardly ever out of New York, and never on the streets?"

Miss Blackman, she looked straight into my eyes, then started to laugh, a rich, low, full laugh. Wasn't till she'd finished, gasping a little, that I got some sense out of her. "Jack, you are not the only orphan in this world. Try to keep that in mind. I may not have been on the streets like you and Mandy, but I've had to look out for myself just the same. You learn. You just learn."

I nodded. I could understand that. "But was it true what you said about the Society? When you give me that nudge in Mrs. Swopes's parlor. Do they really go off saving miscellaneous orphans?"

"You've matured a lot since last winter, young man." She gave me a hard look, as if deciding on something in her head. I guess I got the go-ahead, because she started in, talking slow but steady, looking out across the black wet hills most of the time. "There are truths and there are truths. The real truth is that the Society does send a social worker out to check on its officially placed children on a yearly basis. I knew you and Mandy didn't come under that umbrella, but I tried last night to have Mr. Simmons make an exception. You saw what it was like this morning. Last night was worse. At best, it could be called a stalemate. Me holding up you and Mandy, Mr. Simmons holding up respectability in the form of his nephew."

Red gave a grunt then, so I knew he was listening. Then he butted in. "The boy probably doesn't know what a stalemate is. You want to know what it is, Jack? It's what went on between you and Pie and the Swopes. You wanted Pie to be completely your own, so you wouldn't train him to take to other masters, while Mr. Swopes is set on selling him because he's no use to anyone but you."

I nodded. He had it right there. Guess I had more

stubbornness in me than I figured. I put my eyes back on the track before us and managed to direct the team away from the ditch they were aiming for. But if Simmons and Miss Blackman were a stalemate, and me and Pie was a stalemate, where did that put Miss Blackman and Red? The way they took naturally to each other, but couldn't make their minds meet. They was waltzing around to the selfsame music, if you would of asked my opinion. Course, nobody did.

We settled down to more silence and rain for a while.

We were nearly to the abandoned stone house now, Miss Blackman huddled inside a tent of horse blankets, and Red sheltering under his big Western hat. I'd just ignored the continuing wet, tied up as my mind was between worrying over Mandy and praying the horse trader would outright refuse to buy Pie, so he'd be there for me after. I guessed I'd have to go back to the Swopes, after all. I didn't want to, but wandering around the countryside was getting wearying. And New York hadn't held much glamour for me this last trip. Not even with staying in Red's fancy hotel and going to the theater and eating ice cream. Maybe I'd grown out of the city.

Then we were almost at the crick and Red hadn't said a blessed thing yet about how he intended to get Mandy away.

I hauled back on the reins and stopped the buggy, then bent down to blow out the lantern. "We're getting too close. Hadn't we ought to set up some strategy or something?"

Red looked at me like he was still thinking hard. Me,

I was starting to get het up. These two didn't have any idea at all, at all about the troubles ahead.

"They're not going to just let her go, you know. The Petersons. I can't tell you how rotten they really are."

Red didn't answer, but he took the horse whip out of my hand and jumped down.

"Wait for me," I said, following.

"I'll need to go as well," threw in Miss Blackman, making a move for the edge of the buggy seat.

Suddenly Red came alive. "Never! The boy can come if he wants, but I'll not have you in danger, Angeline. I mean, Miss Blackman. Damn if I will! You'll stay here with the horses until—"

Her eyes sparked up and her back straightened. "What kind of a hothouse flower do you think I am, Mr. Rasmussen?"

It must have been how she said it that set him off, 'cause set off he was. "I'm fed up to my neck and over with following the social conventions you swear by out here in the East. Taken all around, it's already been the longest day of my life. Twenty-four hours on a cattle drive's never been this wearying. And we ain't even done what we've come for yet. I can't take any more of these games we've been playing." He stopped only to catch his breath. "Red. Call me Red, please."

"Only if you call me Angeline." It came out soft, like his words hadn't even angered her.

"If I may take the liberty, it would be an honor."

There they were, starting it up again. I took in the two of them, him standing by the buggy, she staring down, her protective blankets shrugged off.

211

"Just a minute, both of you! You can carry on with the courting after the rescue. But the rescue, that's going to take some planning, because Peterson ain't no fool, and he's a dead shot." I was getting warmed up good now. "Also there's one thing ain't nobody considered yet."

That got their attention.

"What's that, Jack?"

I looked up at Miss Blackman. "What's to be done with Mandy and me after the rescuing is over?"

She looked helpless at that. She didn't have an answer, it was plain.

I turned my eyes to Red. He rubbed at his damp beard like it eased his confusion. "One thing at a time, boy. One thing at a time."

Then all the planning was taken out of our hands. I guess we'd lingered too long on the edge of Peterson's land like that. Must've made more noise than we thought, arguing like we did, too. There was a loud crack, and a rock busted up right next to my boot. I jumped, not knowing what to make of it. The next crack lit on my other side. Then I knew. We was being shot at! I looked up across the crick and saw where the bullets came from by a little puff of white smoke in the dark wet night. Near the barn and sheep paddock.

"Mr. Peterson! Don't shoot! It's me, Jack McConnell, and it's visitors I've brought you!"

"Ain't invited nobody, specially not this time of night. Whoever you be with that mangy boy, you better know you're trespassing! Get off my land, all of you!"

I thought I had him spotted now. Behind the stone wall that penned in his sheep. I looked up to Miss Blackman.

She was still perched on the padded seat, one leg halfway over the side, frozen. I waited for her to pull herself together. Orphan by chance or not, it still took some getting used to, being shot at like that.

But she had grit. "Mr. Peterson? I've just come to see Mandy. A little visit." She slid cautiously off the buggy to the soggy ground. "I'm Miss Blackman, from the Children's Aid Society. I apologize for the hour, but it took all day to get here—"

"Didn't sign no contract. Got no connection with no Children's Aid Society."

He shot again, this time to the left of the Clydesdales. They were not pleased. The two of them started wickering and jerking like they was fixing to take off with the buggy, driver or no. I made a quick leap for the reins that had fallen down over the traces. When I finally had them in hand, I took one more desperate look through the mist rising from the water now, clear across the crick. Was Mandy really still there? Was she still alive? Then something else occurred to me. Where was Red? He'd disappeared when the shooting started. Was he using us as bait to get in closer to Peterson's house and Mandy?

Miss Blackman must have been thinking along the same lines. She raised her voice again, even louder this time, to make sure Peterson could really hear her. Then she started spouting lawyer-like claptrap, just to keep his mind occupied. "In accepting the child from the Bergman family, you became legally part of the transaction, Mr. Peterson. We at Children's Aid are concerned with all defenseless little ones. Orphans are not without rights in our enlightened society—"

If that were only so, I thought to myself, then put my concentration back on trying to track down Red. Was that a slight movement I spotted? Across the crick and over in the scrub bushes to the left of the barn?

"—Children's Aid means just what it says. If she needs help, I've come to give it. Just let me see the girl. Send her out in front of the house, then we'll go away."

Peterson thought about that for a while. Or maybe he was just thinking about all the expensive ammunition he was wasting, and sleep he was losing. Then he let out a yell. "Ma! Send out the orphan brat!"

We waited, me trying to calm the Clydes and my heartbeat, Miss Blackman trying to compose herself again. Finally the door of the shack flung open, a lantern got lit behind it, and Mandy came out into the night, hesitated a little, then came farther toward the crick. Least it had to be Mandy. I hardly recognized her. She was wrapped in rags and limping like a cripple. Mrs. Peterson was trotting behind her, holding out the lantern over Mandy's head so's her little face was lit up like there's a halo around it. Even from this distance, I saw the dark splotches on her face. One eye was all blacked out. I near sat down and bawled.

Peterson, he gave us two minutes to look, then waved his arm for Mandy to go inside again. She started back. Slow, like it was a pain and effort. Then he came from behind the wall right up near her, like he was making sure and certain she obeyed. Satisfied, he aimed his rifle at us straight on. "You seen her. Now git."

I looked up. Miss Blackman nodded. We began turning for the buggy.

Then something happened. Mandy stopped her retreat and spun around, defiance lighting her face, making even the bruises look beautiful. "Jack! Jack, don't come back! He'll hurt you, too! Go now, before—"

But that was all she said. Peterson stepped over and cracked her one on the side of her head with his rifle butt. The sound echoed through the night. Mandy crumpled in front of my eyes.

I could feel that hard wood against her skull like an arrow going clear through my own heart. I flew over the crick and up the little hill, not even thinking that Peterson could turn on me next. It didn't matter. Nothing mattered if Mandy were—

Then there was a sharp snap to my left. My head wavered a moment. Red had come out of hiding just to the rear and one side of Peterson, and he'd hooked that buggy whip clear around the barrel of Peterson's gun. In another second the gun was yanked out of Peterson's grip and tossed aside, the force throwing Peterson backwards onto the ground. I made the final leap for Mandy and picked her up in my arms, rocking her, praying she'd live, numbly waiting for what would happen next.

Red was standing over Peterson with the whip, looking like he was fighting with himself over whether to beat the man into the next world or not. Peterson's face lunged up at him with a combination of ferocity and terror, teeth bared like a mad dog's. I near expected to see the man foaming at the mouth.

Slowly, ever so slowly, Red let the whip slip through his fingers. "I won't do it. I won't give you the satisfaction of the cruelty you deserve." Redbeard stood staring a moment longer, then slowly pulled something out of a pocket. It was his money wallet. Very carefully, he counted out bills, then threw them at Peterson's face. "Here. The price of a good horse. Consider the orphan girl bought and paid for, fair and square."

Then Redbeard turned and walked over to Mandy and me. "She alive, boy?"

I felt Mandy's body tremble ever so gently in my arms. I touched her face. It was wet. From the rain, or my silent tears?

"Yes, sir. I think so."

He reached out and took her from me. "Poor little filly. She found some spunk left, after all. You both did a good job—" He started, but didn't finish. He couldn't see what I could see happening behind his back.

"The gun! Peterson's gone for it again!"

And there was Miss Blackman walking purposefully up from the crick toward us, right into Peterson's line of fire. Peterson didn't seem to notice her at first. He was too busy pointing the gun at us, venting his spleen: "Why the world's so all fired up about one pitiful orphan I'll never know. But the more she's wanted, the more I figure I got me something I ought to keep. So I think I'll just do that."

Miss Blackman was still coming, irregardless of everything. Peterson finally noticed. His gun started to waver a little, like he wasn't sure which target to go for, then he made up his mind and started swinging the rifle toward Miss Blackman.

His finger tightened on the trigger, but I couldn't let him do it. I dove between them, into the shot, willing my body to take it.

When I opened my eyes again, I felt a hot surge of pain that seemed to go all the way through me. It took a moment to realize I wasn't really dying. The pain had a central point, up in my right arm, the arm I'd used as a final shield. I looked around wildly. Redbeard had dropped Mandy and tackled Peterson. Now he had him on the ground again, this time face down. One booted foot was making sure Peterson stayed down. What was Red doing with Peterson's rifle, though? I watched blurry-eyed as he took the stock and broke it clean through over his knee. Then, still not satisfied, Red looked at the barrel a moment before taking it between his two huge fists and slowly— I could almost feel the seconds stop, feel the time stand still—slowly Red bent that gun barrel into a half circle. With only his two hands.

He tossed it aside then, like it weren't nothing, and looked down at Peterson's back. "It's no use trying to talk to a man with neither honor nor the milk of human kindness. I've met wolves and mountain lions I'd trust sooner than you. So I'm just going to hog-tie you now, until I can pick up my casualties and leave. If your woman wants to undo you after we clear out, that's her funeral. If I was her, though, I'd pick up the money you been paid first, then disappear."

Red done like he said, using the buggy whip for rope. It seemed to do the job. Then he walked toward me. "You did even better than I thought, Jack."

He gently lifted me off of the pillow I been bleeding onto. It was Miss Blackman.

"You saved my Angeline. Stubborn woman wouldn't

let well enough alone, wouldn't stay put like I told her."

He was picking her up in his arms now, her body all limp. "Angeline. Speak to me, girl. You can have anything you want. Anything. Just say you won't leave me again!"

I dragged myself nearer to Mandy. Miss Blackman weren't anything but in a dead faint. She'd pull through just fine. I was afraid to think about Mandy, though. I collapsed by her, wondering what to do.

Redbeard finally saw some life in Miss Blackman and set her down again. He stood there, just looking at all of us strewn over the ground, like he didn't know who to start saving first. And in the background there was the sound of the rain, softer now, and a slow keening starting from the Petersons' shack. The lantern was still burning, casting a curious glow over the whole scene from where Mrs. Peterson dropped it when she ran off from Mandy.

Had we rescued Mandy or destroyed her? It looked like one of them Pyrrhic victories. It was desolation pure and simple.

I finally pushed up on my good elbow, dizzy through and through. "You carry Mandy, please. Don't think I can do it."

Red glanced toward the shack. "Anything in there belong to her?"

"The quilt," I said. "Just Mrs. Bergman's quilt." And then I was sliding away myself.

Chapter 14

WHEN NEXT I woke, it was to a place I knew
from somewhere. I'd been here before. I shook the
blinders from my eyes and tried to take it in. There was
a clock over the mantel, ticking now, fancy crockery on
whatnots, big embroidered roses. And Mandy swaddled
up next to me.

The Swopes. We was back in the Swopes' best parlor.
Mandy and me together. That must mean—I turned to
Mandy quick, to see if she was still breathing. Her eyes
flickered open beneath a turban of bandages wrapped
round her head.

"Jack."

They closed again after that whispered prayer, but I
could see she was breathing fine, a little smile on her
face. Thank you, Lord. If nothing else good ever happened
in my life, at least I got Mandy back. That was better
than anything else I could think of. And I wouldn't let
her get away from me again, no sir.

I looked around the parlor again. I guessed us being
there meant it was where we were meant to stay. I thought
about it a while, then decided I could live with it. It

weren't the top, but after what we been through, it ain't the bottom, neither. We'd just bide our time for a few years, then clear out when we were old enough so the world didn't look at us funny. Least I'd have Pie for a few more days. And Peterson shouldn't be bothering us any- more, either. Not after the blow Red gave to his pride. Me, I'd rather be dead and gone than have a man talk to me like Red talked to Peterson. Even if I never saw Red again, I guess he taught me a few things about how a man could fight his battles without guns and blows. A man of honor.

Then the door opened, and two faces peeked in, Miss Blackman and Mrs. Swopes both. They got worried expressions, so I didn't even try to puzzle out what Miss Blackman's still doing there, but forced myself to sit up, to ease their minds.

"Fit as a fiddle—" But the blood rushed up to my head dreadful, and I could see I wasn't.

Then they were both hurrying in, fussing over me.

Me and Mandy, we both lost us another day or two, until we was setting by the Swopes' kitchen table next to each other, trying to piece things together. Miss Blackman, she was dressed up in one of Mrs. Swopes's old aprons, pitch- ing in with the kitchen work like she was born to it. Mrs. Swopes was smiling and talking like she come out of a long sleep. They was trying to get more broth into Mandy and me. I couldn't take any more.

"Where's Redbeard?"

"Red's gone into New Hope, dear." It was Miss Black- man, lighting up over his name like old times. "To pick up some medicine from the doctor for the two of you."

"Oh." Looked like they'd made up. They'd probably be getting married any day now, then heading West. And me and Mandy would be left with the Swopes, like I'd figured. I'd already planned on sticking it out. Still, it pained a little.

"After the . . . the accidents, we had to get you two to a warm place fast. Essie here was kind enough to give us shelter. It probably saved your lives." She gave Mrs. Swopes an appreciative look.

"It wasn't nothing, Angeline. No more than my Christian duty. Don't hurt Clifford and Amos none to sleep in the attic a few days to make room for you. And just to listen to you talking about New York City has done a wonder for me. It almost felt like I been walking down that there Fifth Avenue, looking at them fine shops and mansions, dressed up like a gentlewoman myself."

The two of 'em beamed at each other some more.

Then Mandy pushed her own bowl away. "Will Jack and I be staying in the attic again, then? After Miss Blackman leaves? Can we whitewash it like you promised before?"

Mrs. Swopes looked a little flustered. "Well now, dear, you know I'd be pleased as punch to have both of you back here permanent, but—"

Miss Blackman took over. "But Red and I thought that, after all you two have been through, you might like to have a say in the matter yourselves."

Mandy asked, in a puzzled voice, "You mean we have a choice?"

"Yes, Mandy dear, you have a choice. You've earned

it. And we'll discuss it when Red gets back. Together."

Mandy and I gave each other a look. An unbelieving look. Ain't nobody ever give us a choice before. It was do this, or do that, go here or go there, irregardless of anything. What might the choices be, I wondered. Then I looked at my arm in its sling, and Mandy's head all bandaged up like it was. What kind of choices do people give two youngsters as beat up and wore out as we was? We sure as certain wasn't up to much manual labor for a while, and I couldn't see Mr. Swopes wasting food on us till we was back in form. Not if we chose to go. Now Essie, Mrs. Swopes, that is, she was a different matter entire since Miss Blackman arrived. She didn't look like she'd grudge the two of us anything anymore.

Hoofbeats coming into the yard broke my chain of concentration. I eased off the chair by the table, gently, so as not to jostle my arm, and headed for the door. "It's Redbeard. Got to be. I'll tell him we're fine. We're ready to talk."

I already got the door opened and cold air is blasting into the kitchen. Autumn must of come on strong whilst Mandy and I been recovering. Then I see it isn't Redbeard at all, but some rough-shaven man, mustaches drooping clear down to his jowls, leading a string of horses.

"Who is it?"

We're all at the door now, staring out. It was Mrs. Swopes who spoke up.

"Why, that's never Mr. Rasmussen. It's Clem Cuttlebert, the horse trader. Fe-lix!"

But she needn't of yelled like that, 'cause there was Mr. Swopes and the boys turning out of the barn fast. And there was my Pie, his nose poked over the paddock fence, curious about the excitement.

Pie. My heart sunk again. Now I knew for sure why people took to churchgoing so. Just when you thought you had everything fixed up right, along come something else to pull your feet out from under you. There weren't no heaven on this earth, so there surely needed to be one up above. Maybe someday I'd have Pie up there in the sky with me. But for right now, he was almost gone.

I turned. "Where's my jacket? What've you done with my jacket?"

"Whatever is the matter, Jack? You can't go out there yet!"

"They're about to sell off my horse, Miss Blackman. I got to say goodbye to him."

They found my jacket, then Mandy wanted to come, too, but the women wouldn't let her, not with her concussion. Her strength wasn't near up to mine yet.

I raced across the yard to the paddock, and was heaving and aching till I got to where Pie was waiting for me. Then I had my good arm up around his neck and was talking to him. "I said it before, and it's still true. I tried the best I could for you, Pie. But maybe I done it the wrong way. If I'd known then what a stalemate was, I would've trained you for the Swopes boys, too. Now it's too late. Now I've got to say goodbye, and I haven't even a carrot to give you. You try to be good now, and maybe someone decent'll buy you. Maybe I'll be able to find you someday, when I've got money saved, and take you out West, set you free like I promised . . ."

He was nuzzling at me now, whinnying in my ear. I couldn't go on. I looked up and saw Swopes and the trader coming over to us.

"This is a fine animal," Swopes started in. "Got papers on him and everything. The boy here tamed him his own self from wild. Still got a little too much spirit, but nothing that can't be beat out of him."

The trader pushed up next to me and took Pie's mouth in his hands, pulling away his lips to inspect his teeth.

"He's young, you can see that, Clem. Not more'n three, four years old. He's got a good, long, useful life ahead of him. And look at his flanks there, even give the Lord pleasure in the strength of them."

"You trying to sell me a horse or a Bible, Swopes?"

But that trader, he looked over Pie real good. Finally he stopped looking. "Give you fifty-five for him, Swopes."

"Now, look here, Clem. This animal ain't ready for a tannery yet. He's got racing blood. You can do better'n that. He's worth at least a hunderd."

"If he can't be tamed to a harness, he's just another horse, Swopes."

Mr. Swopes, he drew himself up tall. "A spirited horse, Clem Cuttlebert. Spirited!"

The trader, he humphed and spit a little, then: "Seventy-five. That's as far as I'll go."

"Make it eighty-five and you've got a deal. The price of milk was down this year, and the hail didn't do no good to my crops."

That trader made faces like it was paining him worse than my shot-up arm and spit again. Finally: "Eighty, and not a nickel more. Bring him out."

Well, I jumped down from the fence and started slinking back to the house. I couldn't bear it to watch Pie took off like that. Then I heard another sound. More horses coming? It was a team. The buggy, carrying Redbeard. I didn't stop to think, I just ran straight for him.

Redbeard, he pulled up fast, maybe a foot before the buggy wheels ran me down. "What are you doing out of bed, Jack? You're not near fit enough yet!"

"Red. Sir! Swopes, he's just sold off my horse!"

"What's this?"

And Redbeard jumped down and went storming over to where they were trying to catch Pie in the paddock, but not having much luck, because he was shying and kicking mud all over them.

"What's going on here, Swopes?"

"Ain't nothing going on but my business. Just sold me a horse to Clem here."

"It's the boy's horse you sold!"

"Might've thought it was his, but the horse was my property, right enough. Only now it's Clem's. If he can catch him. Just paid me in cold cash for him."

Redbeard stopped right there and turned to the trader. "You the owner now?"

I could almost see the trader's mustaches start to curl up at his new turn of luck. "Yes, sir. Indeed I am. Fine piece of horseflesh, got racing possibilities."

"Don't care what it is. Belongs on my ranch, and I'll have it." Then Redbeard was digging for his money pouch again. "How much you pay Swopes for it?"

"Eighty! Eighty dollars!" I couldn't help but butt in at that point.

"Fair enough. Here's ninety. The day's still young and already you made yourself a good profit."

Clem Cuttlebert, he looked like he just swallowed a bowl of cream, and Swopes like it was cream stolen from under his own nose. Redbeard didn't pay any of it no mind. He just turned to me. "If you're this fit, then it's time to be moving on. Go gather Mandy and Miss Blackman in the parlor. We've got some discussing to do."

The door to the parlor was shut, and Mandy and I were balanced on the sofa, me fussing with the key still around my neck. Red was leaning against the mantel again, like he was growing there, and Miss Blackman was doing some dignified pacing over the carpet. If I thought making choices was easy, I had another thought coming. It wasn't that Mandy and I couldn't make up our minds, it was the grownups at it again. Maybe they hadn't made up as completely as I'd figured.

Miss Blackman was talking right now. "I brought enough money with me to buy train tickets for myself and the children back to New York."

Red shuffled his feet once, then leaned against the wall again. "What'll you do with 'em back in New York?"

That gave Miss Blackman pause. She looked at us. "I'm not sure. Perhaps Mr. Simmons and the Society will forgive my brief lapse of decorum and take me back. That would give me an income suitable to supporting all of us modestly. Very modestly." She stopped. "The children could get some education, and help out around the building, like I did when I was their age."

"The city of New York ain't any place to be raising a

boy like Jack here. Nor Mandy, either. They've both of them got too much spirit. They belong where the country is open and free. They belong in a place too big for small minds." He stopped to give us a look, then threw in the clincher. "Besides which, I just paid good money for a racehorse which is no earthly use without its trainer. Now, when you add in the price of freighting that horse all the way back to Nebraska, well . . . It just don't make good sense, does it?"

What was Red up to, anyway? Here was a man wouldn't think twice about throwing away his hard-earned cash on confidence men and the like, fussing about Pie's freight bill to go West. I nudged Mandy, to get her attention, but found it was elsewhere. She was staring at the two of them fixedly. Looked like she was about to come out with a doozy.

"I never met Miss Blackman before my rescue," she started, "but Jack, well, Jack told me lots about you, ma'am. When I opened my eyes in this very parlor after being sick, I first saw Jack, so I guessed I was all right. The next time I opened my eyes, it was Miss Blackman I saw. Then I knew I was all right, but it was heaven I'd gone to. You're like the angel on the ceiling from our old house, ma'am. The one Jack and I stayed in last winter. I'd dearly love to live with you." She stopped. "But no matter what happens from now on, I know I have to stay with Jack. Things are always fine when I'm with Jack."

She gave me one of her smiles. Least she let me off on the flapping eyelashes. But I thought I knew what she was leading up to. I let her get it all out.

"I know Jack loves me, but he loves his horse, too. I

227

guess that means we'll have to go with the horse out West, since Mr. Redbeard is offering." She looked around the parlor. "Mrs. Swopes was nice, but I think I'm tired of Pennsylvania. And New York."

"But, Mandy," I broke in. "Mandy! Don't you remember all our talks about a real home? I don't think we ought to choose for anything but a *real* home. With a real mother and father!"

That started Red up from the wall. "Are you saying I wouldn't make a fine father, Jack?"

"No offense meant, Red, sir. You're the right age, and I do admire you—" This was harder getting out than I thought. "But a real home ought to have a mother, too. And love. Everybody caring for each other. Mandy and I, we worked out all the necessaries in our minds. But since you and Miss Blackman can't seem to make up your minds—"

Now Mandy took over. "Why can't you make up your minds, anyhow? Anyone can see that you're crazy about each other. Why can't you get married? Then we'd have a *real* home."

Miss Blackman stopped her pacing, and Red retreated back to the mantel again.

"See what happens when you give a child a choice, Angeline? They get all uppity like this."

"Are you really sure you want to take on the fathering of two uppity children, Red?"

"Only if I've got you to take on the mothering, Angeline."

"You know by now how I truly feel about you, Red. But it's not something I can do on the spur of the moment.

I've got apologies to make back in New York, obligations to sort through. And you like everything done *now*, this instant."

Red was standing on his own feet again. "I don't work like namby-pamby New York men, Angeline, and I never will. Out West, a man has to learn to act fast. When the sudden snows come, he has to know how to save his cattle. When a rattler lunges up, he has to have his gun ready to shoot. He has to be decisive. I know my courting hasn't been what you're used to, and I apologize for that, but I knew what I wanted first time I laid eyes on you. That won't ever change for me."

"Oh, Red, I wouldn't want that part of you to change, nor any other, either—"

"Then you do love me."

She blushed. Mandy and I looked at each other, then the four of us were smiling and laughing. It might take a little time, but it was going to work out all right, sure enough.

"Come on, Mandy," I said. "Let's get packed up. We're going home."